SHADOWS ACROSS THE WATER

Heartbroken after her fiancé, Jake Buchanan, is believed drowned, Blythe Neilsen leaves her home on Australia's longest river to escape the memories. A year later, she returns to care for her ailing father, and is supported by Jake's older brother, Nat, who now runs the family's paddle steamer business. Slowly, Blythe recaptures her love of the river, but her life is again thrown into turmoil when she comes face to face with the truth.

Books by Jo James
in the Linford Romance Library:

CHANCE ENCOUNTER
THE RELUCTANT BACHELOR

JO JAMES

SHADOWS ACROSS THE WATER

Complete and Unabridged

LINFORD
Leicester

First published in Great Britain in 2000

First Linford Edition
published 2004

British Library CIP Data

James, Jo

James, J
Shad Shadows across   int ed.—
Linfo the water / Jo
1. Lo James
2. La
I. Titl   ROM LP
823.9
      1569197

ISBN 1–84395–268–8

Published by
F. A. Thorpe (Publishing)
Anstey, Leicestershire

Set by Words & Graphics Ltd.
Anstey, Leicestershire
Printed and bound in Great Britain by
T. J. International Ltd., Padstow, Cornwall

This book is printed on acid-free paper

1

Blythe Neilsen hadn't been home for more than twelve months, not since Jake had disappeared a week before they were to be married. It took her pa's sudden illness to bring her back.

As she neared the bridge across Australia's longest river, she eased her foot off the accelerator, and, turning into a clearing on the cliffside, parked her hatchback. Forcing herself from the car, she stared down into the Murray's waters. The river rippled and shimmered in the early winter sunshine, temporarily blinding her. How peaceful it looked, how much in harmony with the sweep and colour of the landscape. Yet these were the same unpredictable, treacherous waters which had taken Jake away from her. She shuddered, asked herself again the question. Why? What had gone so terribly wrong that he chose to end his life instead of marry her?

Into her unhappy thoughts came a tuneful, merry whistle — once, twice, three times. She started, glanced at her watch. Close on four o'clock. The paddle steamer, the Becky Em, named after her grandmother, must be close by. Soon it would appear around the bend, splitting the waters with its bow, and then it would rock and sway into the quay, to be tied up for the day. Her thoughts ran on. The tourists would spill from it, laughing, happy. Nat Buchanan would doff his captain's hat, with the words Becky Em worked across it, say he hoped they'd enjoyed their trip, and would come again.

Blythe turned away, and flopped back into her car. Protecting her right to be unhappy, she cradled the memories of Jake to her.

She and Jake had put off marriage, saved and planned excitedly for the day when they could afford their own river boat. They'd turn it into a cruise boat to take tourists on week-long trips to the Murray's mouth in South Australia. But when the river took Jake, it also took part of her. She hated its majesty, its power.

She fumbled the key in the ignition, the engine thrummed into life, and bracing herself, she drove over the bridge, a modern concrete edifice. Beside it, the old timber structure rotted in the heat and occasional floods, waiting to be rescued from the bureaucrats by the local historical society.

It had waited now for years, as she had waited these last twelve months for the truth about Jake's disappearance to be found. She gave a short, cynical laugh. In her heart she knew it wouldn't happen. Jake had left a suicide note. The authorities and the family accepted he had undressed on the river's edge and walked into its depths. There was nothing for the police to probe, as yet no coroner's inquest, no body.

Both Pa and Nat had advised her not to hope.

'Go away for a while, Blythe. You're twenty-four. You've got the rest of your life in front of you. In Sydney you could make a fresh start, get a job, make some new friends,' Nat said.

'But I can't leave you, Pa.'

'You can still come home for weekends and holidays,' Pa had replied, laughing as he added, 'and if you're worried about me, love, I'm as fit as a trout.'

Nat had put his arm around the old man's shoulders.

'We're mates, aren't we, Tom? We'll be fine, Blythe. You need to get away from here, at least for a while.'

She took his advice. He was her loved and trusted older foster brother. She had no siblings of her own, her brother, Rohan, having died at birth.

But Sydney had been a mistake. She saw no beauty in its harbour, in the shadows of its waters, the frenetic hoot and dash of ferries as they transported commuters and visitors back and forth. She moved to a town beyond the city.

There she found a job as a computer programmer in a small hospital, a comfortable, little flat, and a circle of new friends. She was beginning to get herself together. And then the phone call about Pa's illness came.

Her car now left the other side of the bridge. She was in Victoria, home. It looked the same, but arriving after a trip no longer made her heart leap or filled her with joy. A tear fell on to her hand, which was clasped tightly around the steering wheel. Irritated with herself, she dashed it away. She had to have control over her tears now. She had to be cheerful and positive for Pa.

She stopped again in town, bought a newspaper, a cheap paperback, some bread rolls in the busy plaza, delaying her homecoming, the greetings. Finally, the sun disappeared, the day grew chilly. She could put it off no longer.

Driving the car along a back road, and taking a side street, she avoided the curve of the river before pulling into the driveway of Pa's house. It faced the river, separated from it by a wide, bitumen road and a grassy slope. The house was old, single-storeyed, rendered brick of the Thirties, but substantial, spacious and comfortable. Blythe knew every room, where every piece of antique furniture sat, solid, enduring, as she always thought her Pa to be, until now.

The garden, set on a generous piece of land, looked well-tended, the lawns clipped. It was covered in part by an ageing carpet of autumn leaves from the giant golden elm. Everything seemed normal. Nothing indicated Pa's illness. She set back her shoulders, breathed in, was about to place her key in the door when it swung open. Nat Buchanan's tanned faced crinkled with a wide smile.

'Blythe!'

Pain stormed through her. The voice could almost have been Jake's. Nat reached out with strong, bronzed arms and held her close to his chest.

'How's my little sister?' he asked.

The stiffness of the epaulette of his captain's shirt grazed her chin. When Jake had worn a similar shirt, it had brushed against her skin, too. Tears gathered in her eyes. Would she ever forget the feeling of being in Jake's arms?

Nat reminded her so much of her love. Though six years older, he had the same dark hair, the same wide fore-head, the same harmony of nose, lips, lean cheekbones. The difference was in their height and their eyes. Nat was taller, more muscular and his eyes were dark, serious. Jake's had been an exceptional, luminous blue, resonant with energy and life. They were the first thing you noticed about him.

'Your eyes dance like Puck's in A Midsummer-Night's Dream. They sparkle with mischief,' she told him after they fell in love.

He'd laughed.

'Aren't you forgetting I played Oberon, King of the Fairies, in the school play?'

'You should have been Puck. You were miscast.'

'You, too. You should have been Titania, Queen of the Fairies, not the insignificant little fairy, Mustard Seed.'

'Your brother always said I was very well cast, considering my temper. Anyway, whoever heard of a fairy queen with brown eyes,' she'd said with a satisfied smirk and a toss of her then short, dark hair.

No-one but Jake could have equated her with a queen of fairies. No delicate little figure, no long fair curls or rosebud mouth for her.

Now she felt Nat's hands on her shoulders.

'Hey, Blythe, tears? Not much of a greeting for big brother who's been sweating on your arrival.'

His large hand dipped into the pocket of his trousers. He drew out a handkerchief, unfolded it and offered it to her.

'Thanks,' she choked, a lump in her throat, then she blew her nose, gained a

8

little composure. 'So, what are you doing here?' she managed to ask.

'Where else would I be? I'll always be here for the man who gave me and Jake a chance in life. After every river trip, I report to Tom how it went, how many tourists came aboard, what money we took. That's my excuse for hanging around. I daren't let him know I'm really checking up on him, keeping an eye on things. He's so damned set on not being a burden to anyone.'

His fingers curled into the soft flesh of her arm. He didn't know his own strength.

'I'm glad you're here, Blythe. You know he'd never ask anyone for help. I should warn you, though, he doesn't know I suggested you come home. He thinks you decided it was time.'

Blythe should have felt grateful to this man, but he succeeded only in making her feel guilty, and in her present mood, she resented it.

'Don't you think you should have asked him first?' she said shortly, freeing herself from his hold. 'He mightn't want me.'

'He wants you all right. He's over the moon. You should have seen his tired, old eyes light up when I said you'd rung and were on your way.'

'I hope you didn't say it was permanent. I've only got a week's break.'

'I'm sorry if I've done the wrong thing. I didn't say you were here for good, but . . . '

She sighed heavily.

'But he presumed it, and you didn't bother to put him straight.'

Her voice rose. Nothing was going right.

'Sh! Let's not get into that now. He's waiting for you in his best bib and tucker. I tried to persuade him to wear his old captain's hat.'

Nat was trying to cheer her up, to put the best light on things. He'd always been the family peacemaker. Sometimes, after she and Jake had an argument, even a small disagreement,

10

he'd step in to patch up things. At the time it annoyed her because somehow it made her feel immature, naïve.

She used to chip him, 'Nat Buchanan, one day I'm going to nominate you for the Nobel Peace Prize.'

'Or sainthood,' Jake would chime in. 'Saint Nathaniel. Hey, I like that, eh?'

He'd laugh. Blythe could hear his laughter. She came close to slapping her hands over her ears to close out the sound.

Before she turned into the second door on the right, she drew in a long breath, trying to restore her composure. This had always been the sitting room, the place where the family gathered at night and on special occasions. Here, the flames of a fire sparked and jigged on cold, frosty evenings, and the air-conditioner rumbled relentlessly during the hot, endless days from spring into autumn.

Today the last of the rays of early winter sunshine filtered through the window. Pa sat in its warmth, pale. As she entered, a smile touched his thin lips.

'Blythe,' he whispered.

She strained to hear his voice and moved closer.

'How are you, my little Chilli,' he said.

She rushed to him, kneeled beside him, picked up his hand.

'Your little Chilli is fine. You haven't called me that in a long time.'

Nat had christened her Chilli because as he said, 'Blythe is such a toffy name, and it doesn't suit someone with a little temper like yours, Miss Neilsen.'

'She's high-spirited, like her father, and she has to compete with you boys and her pa. Good luck to her, I say,' Gran had defended her, but the name stuck and she even grew fond of it.

In the end everyone in the household called her Chilli or Hot Chilli, depending on her moods, until she turned twenty-one.

'It's banned from now on. I've grown

up. Left my bad temper behind,' she'd declared at the family celebration.

It raised a chorus of disbelieving laughter, but after that there were only occasional lapses, like now. Her eyes shimmering with tears, she kissed Pa.

'Are you doing everything the doctor ordered, or are you being your usual independent self?'

He nodded and tears welled in his faded eyes.

'My usual independent self, what else?' he said, his voice no more than a murmur. 'I'm glad you're home, love.'

A knot twisted in her stomach.

'All that is going to change while little Chilli is around to see that you do as you're told. I'm hot stuff, remember.'

She tried to joke with him, to sound definite, confident, as she rose unsteadily to her feet.

'Are you warm enough? Can I get you a cup of tea?'

'I'll get it. You stay with Tom. Weak black tea for you, Blythe?' Nat said from somewhere in the background.

'You don't have to. I can do it,' she insisted.

Tom reached out, touched her arm.

'Nat won't mind. Stay by me for a while. We can talk. It's been so long.'

Blythe had driven for six hours from Sydney. She longed for a shower, to lie on her bed, to sleep, to forget this nightmare.

'Thank you, Nat. Do you know where everything is?'

'Of course he does. He moved back in a while ago. Not much point him keeping up his house, and me here on my own. Besides, it's easier for him to report in, now I can't get down to the Becky Em.'

Blythe shot Nat a hard glance.

'You're staying here?' she snapped. 'You didn't bother to mention it earlier.'

'Naturally I'll move back to my own place now you've arrived. I understand I won't be needed.'

He swung away and left the room. She heard his footfall on the polished boards, felt glad to have him gone, but guilty for being so testy. Excusing herself with Pa, she hurried to the kitchen. Nat was filling the kettle when she approached.

'I'm sorry. I sound like a spoiled, ungrateful brat. I don't know why. You've been so generous. Clearly you let Pa think it suited you to move in. It probably didn't.'

'Hush up,' he said, switching on the kettle. 'You're tired. A cup of tea and you'll be a new woman.'

'Ha, ha,' she said mockingly. 'Aren't you forgetting the aspirin that goes with the cup of tea?'

'And the good lie down, as I remember it,' he said evenly. 'Would you prefer coffee? It might help keep you awake.'

She laid her hand on his strong arm, and as quickly drew it away. He reminded her too much of Jake, stirred latent feelings. Her voice broke.

'Forgive me, Nat? Friends?'

Nat felt relieved.

'Friends,' he repeated.

It occurred to him that the dull eyes she turned on him questioned why he lived, when Jake, his younger brother, the man she loved so deeply, was dead. If only they didn't have similar features. If only he'd thought to grow a beard, or get his head shaved, buy a pair of rimless glasses, anything to spare her the pain of looking at him, remembering Jake, anything to stop her turning away from him, her pain-filled eyes, puzzled, or glistening with tears. He didn't blame her. He just felt useless.

'Did you say coffee?'

She sat on a kitchen chair.

'Nat,' she faltered.

He guessed what was coming.

'Is there any news? Have there been any . . . er . . . developments?'

'You'd have been the first to know, but unfortunately, no. It's a year now. Please try not to hang on to the idea that Jake will turn up one day, Blythe. He's gone, sweetheart. You have to come to terms with that. I have.'

'But I don't understand it. If we'd found him, if we could have had a funeral, if I could have said farewell, I might have stopped grieving. As it is I still keep hoping.'

Her restless fingers ran through her long hair. The spread of sunlight from the window highlighted the coppery threads in the thick, dark cap of hair. When she once had it cut, Jake had called her a tomboy.

'What's wrong with that?' she'd demanded. 'I want to drive the paddle steamer anyway,' and she'd plopped on Tom's captain's hat.

It fell to her ears. They'd all laughed. Nat remembered it in detail, yet it seemed a lifetime ago.

'I've wondered sometimes — would it help if we organised a memorial service?' Nat asked.

She shook her head, looked up at him with a poignancy which tore at his heart.

'That would be so final. Nat, why would he kill himself? We'd waited so long, but we were to be married in a week's time. Everything was booked. Do you think he changed his mind? That he didn't love me after all? You knew him better than anyone. What do you really think?'

She wept quietly. He wanted to go to her, to hold her, but he wasn't Jake.

'Yes, I knew him best, and he loved you, Blythe. Never doubt it. Who knows how the mind works? Maybe he just got confused. He'd arranged to buy the Rosina. Maybe in the end he realised he didn't really want a life on the river. He did have some doubts, you know.'

She drew the handkerchief he'd given her earlier from the pocket of her jeans, mopped away at her eyes, her face.

'Who told you that?' she protested. 'It's not true. He would have told me. Besides, it doesn't make any sense. The idea of buying the Rosina was mine, but he said he was as keen as me.'

'I'm not putting any of the blame down to you, but once or twice he mentioned the commitment, how the

18

bank loan would tie him down.'

Nat searched for answers which might satisfy her.

'If only Jake had gone on to university he could have been anything in the media. Perhaps he regretted not doing that.'

How could he explain to her when he didn't understand it himself? He placed a mug of coffee in front of her.

'Drink,' he commanded, 'and stop punishing yourself.'

Her fingers cradled her cup.

'Maybe he regretted me.'

She took a hasty sip of coffee, then drew the mug away quickly as if it had burned her lips.

'Blythe, he loved you. He wanted a life with you.'

'But not enough, it seems. If only he hadn't left that suicide note. Could someone else have written it?'

'You saw it. You know his handwriting. What's your opinion?'

She shrugged.

'But don't you ever think Jake will

walk in one day? I do. I have this feeling that he's still alive, somewhere. I still look for him around every corner, in every crowd.'

She choked back a sob. They'd been down this track again and again before she left for Sydney. And they seemed destined to repeat it over and over, until she finally believed Jake was dead. If only they'd discovered his body, she could have done her grieving — they all could have — and moved forward.

'Sure, I sometimes have a prickly feeling he's standing next to me, telling me to get a life. For a while there I sometimes thought I heard him coming home late, putting his key in the door. They say that's natural when two people have been very close. But it's twelve months now, Blythe. Jake's probably organising the annual canoe marathon in Heaven.'

Not a flicker of a smile touched her lips.

'He may have been tricked into writing that note. I suppose you didn't think of that, Nat Buchanan?' she snapped.

'Sure he liked playing the occasional practical joke on others, but he was too smart to be the victim of one. Anyway, I ran the idea by the police, just in case. They didn't think it had any merit.'

'What if he lost his memory and wandered off?'

'After writing that note?' Nat said, trying to be patient. 'He'd have been located by now. Look, we'd better get back to Tom. He'll be thinking we went out for a takeaway coffee. If you want, we can talk again, after dinner, once Tom's settled for the night.'

Jake's suicide had come as a huge shock to him, too. He knew his brother's weaknesses and strengths better than anyone, but the police had looked into it and accepted that Jake had walked into the murky river after wandering down to its banks following a night of pre-wedding drinking with mates.

Nat's mind travelled back to the time

when Tom had found Jake and Nat as boys, sleeping on the anchored, ageing paddle steamer, which later became the Becky Em. They'd fled the strict confines of their foster parents, who had three children of their own.

'Don't send us back, Captain Tom. Why can't we live on the boat? I could help you repair it and get it working again. I'm nearly seventeen,' Nat had pleaded. 'The Richeys treat us like slaves. Poor little Jake gave some lip the other day and he got a terrible thrashing. They've done it before, too. That's why we cleared out.'

Tom and Becky, who'd lost their son and his wife in a road accident and were already caring for their granddaughter, Blythe, formalised arrangements with the child welfare authorities, and the courts, to foster the boys. Nat had won a scholarship to university, where he studied marine engineering. As Jake grew up, he became the promotions man for the restored paddle steamer. On board, he welcomed the tourists, stocked the snack and souvenir shop, served the complimentary wine from the local vineyards, kept the visitors entertained with stories, played his guitar and sang. People gravitated to him.

Though they loved their new family, fitted in, the two boys remained close to each other. Jake had always turned first to Nat when things got tough.

'Nat, did you hear me?' Blythe's voice cut through his reminiscing.

He pushed back the sleeve of his shirt.

'You were saying?'

'I was thanking you for listening to me, but apparently you weren't. Anyway, I'm through talking today. I have to get myself together for Pa's sake.'

Blythe could lose it occasionally, living up to her nickname, Chilli. Soon she got over her moods, but since her arrival Nat noticed a sharp, hard edge to her voice, to her manner. Everything he said seemed to spark another wave of irritation.

'OK, let's get back to him before he sends out a search party.'

His over-generous laugh didn't impress her either, for she raised her brows, picked up a laden tea tray and stalked off. Behind her, he noticed she'd lost weight. She looked like model material in her close-fitting jeans, her skimpy little top. He hoped she hadn't got into bad eating habits.

As she turned back to him, his glance quickly reverted from her figure to her face.

'There's really no need for you to stay on, now I'm here. I'm sure you're anxious to get back to your own place,' she said.

'Sure, but there are some things you should know about Tom's medication and routine, and you'll need my help getting him to bed.'

'I'm not stupid. I'll manage. Leave me the instructions.'

She wasn't stupid, just terribly

unhappy. Her dark eyes, the tightness of her wide mouth said everything. If only he could put the sparkle back in those eyes.

'Come on, Blythe, let's see you smile, for Tom. He needs you.'

'I'll do what I can. Thanks again for reminding me, Nat.'

Her mouth curved gently. The smile didn't reach her eyes, but at least she was trying. She shivered.

'It's starting to get chilly. Is a frost forecast for tonight?'

'You should have something warmer on, but I'll light the fire. We light it early because Tom feels it, the minute the sun disappears.'

In the sitting room, Nat rubbed his hands together.

'Time for a fire, Tom?'

Nat bent towards the already set fire, put a match to the paper and kindling. It crackled and sparked as it flared into life. Behind him, he was conscious of Blythe pouring tea for Tom, heard the rattle of the cup as he took it in shaky hands, his murmur of, 'Thanks, little Chilli,' her attempt at a laugh. He decided that while he stuck around, he'd be in the way of Tom and Blythe getting close again, really talking. He stood up.

'Well, folks, I'm out of here. I've got the book work to record, and later some friends to catch up with.'

Tom's face creased in a smile.

'He means a special friend, love. He's been seeing the widow Savage a lot lately.'

Startled, Blythe looked up sharply.

'Jenny? You're seeing Jenny Savage?'

He nodded.

'Sure. She's been a good friend these last months.'

'A real good friend, I reckon.'

Tom tried to laugh, but it made him wheeze. Blythe didn't feel like laughing, not one little bit, and she wasn't sure why. But it had something to do with her never having to share Nat with anyone. He'd always been there, solely for her.

2

For the first time, it occurred to Blythe that Nat had never shown interest in a woman before. She'd come to think of him as kind of belonging to her family. Besides, he didn't seem to need a lady. His was a love affair with engines. When you thought about Nat you pictured him either in overalls stained with grease, or his captain's uniform, self-sufficient, a man who knew exactly where he was going in life.

When he talked it centred around the Becky Em and how fantastic the early pioneers were who built her; how in those days, the beautiful, wood-fired furnace drove the paddles, propelled the steamer. He'd gesture with big, capable hands, a tanned, well-muscled body and explain why he'd replaced it with a diesel engine, and how efficiently that engine ran.

When it came to social conversation, at parties you'd find him in a corner, surrounded by a group of admiring younger men, talking ships and the river. Occasionally she'd locate him in the solitude of someone's bedroom, thumbing through an engineering journal. But with her, he was always comfortable, because he regarded her as a sister. As she grew up, he encouraged her to take her problems to him rather than worry her ageing Pa. She had no qualms about confiding in him, for any secrets they shared remained locked safely away in his memory bank — except that one time. She'd asked him if he thought Jake cared for her as a woman, and he'd replied, a glint in his eyes, 'You're falling in love with him, aren't you, Chilli?'

She'd tugged at her bottom lip with her teeth, and finally admitted in a hushed voice, 'I've loved him for years. Oh, Nat, what should I do? He doesn't care for me like that.'

His dark eyes had appraised her gently.

'You don't have to do anything. I'm sure he loves you, too. You'll see, he'll make a move soon.'

And within days, Jake had asked her out to dinner at the poshest restaurant in town. Nat had apparently told Jake about her feelings, but it didn't trouble her. Without a nudge, he might never have noticed her as a woman. The younger Buchanan was sought all over town to be master of ceremonies at the local dances, do a running commentary at the annual canoe races and river carnivals, pursued by the females for his thirst for adventure, his fun-loving personality, his generous smile, and best of all, those blue, heart-stopping eyes. And yet, he'd chosen her.

On that first date, he'd ordered for her from a French menu she didn't understand. After the waiter left, he'd grinned.

'We're starting with frogs' legs, followed by snails.'

She'd giggled.

'I always thought you were a bit crazy. Now I know it. If you think I won't eat them, forget it.'

The waiter brought grilled steak topped by a mushroom sauce and vegetables. She picked over her dinner with her fork.

'So where are the snails and frogs' legs? Explain yourself, Jake Buchanan.'

His blue eyes gleamed.

'Any other girl would have shrieked and raced out.'

'I'm not any other girl.'

'I'm just starting to realise that. I'm not interested in ordinary girls, anyway.'

On their next date, he'd toasted her in champagne.

'To the Queen of the Fairies,' he'd said, as he linked his arm through hers, and they clicked their stemmed crystal flutes together by candlelight, and drank.

He'd taken her hand, stroked it with sensual fingers. They'd moved on to the small dance floor, and in its subdued lighting, he'd drawn her close. She'd rested her chin on his shoulder, and slowly they'd circled to the music.

'You're my girl now, aren't you?' he'd whispered as they'd walked to the river, their arms wrapped around one another.

On the sandy beach by its edge, he kissed her. Blythe had moved into a vast new world, where everything she did, every decision she made was coloured by her adoration of Jake. Tears stung Blythe's eyes now, her memories of those dates vivid, achingly real.

'Chilli and I insist you stay for dinner. Go out later, if you've promised Jenny.'

Blythe started. Was Tom speaking to her? She forced herself back to the present.

'Of course, we insist,' she said automatically.

'Later we'll yarn about the old days, the good times, and Nat can fill you in on the little business. We're partners now,' Tom wheezed.

'Partners? Lovely,' she mumbled vaguely, intent on hiding her misty eyes from Pa.

He mustn't know his impetuous little Chilli had lost her fire. After more than a year she'd made progress, but returning home had dragged her back to the beginning of her story-book romance with Jake, and its cruel ending. She straightened her back as Nat helped Tom to position the oxygen mask over his face. It was attached to the cylinder by his chair.

'I should be doing more for you. I wish there was something positive I could do, Pa. I hate seeing you so weak. It's not fair.'

His hand patted hers. It felt so cold. She tried not to shiver.

'There, there, you're here now love. Stay a while. That's all I ask.'

She sank on to the rug at his feet, stretched her arms towards the fire, and felt warm for the first time since she'd arrived at the outskirts of Murray Bend. For Pa's sake, she forced herself to think of happier times, and soon the tightness in her stomach eased.

'When you bought the old paddle steamer, no-one in town believed you'd ever get it going, let alone turn it into a successful business. They were exciting times, Pa,' she began.

'No-one but me,' Nat put in and Blythe realised she'd forgotten Nat was there. 'I always saw the possibilities.'

'You were an integral part of the plan, son.'

Pa dragged off the oxygen mask, his voice becoming stronger, as if the memory provided the stimulus.

'And now you're running it, keeping the dream alive. I don't know what I'd have done without this man, Chilli, especially after your gran died. He's rock solid. And when I go, you'll be partners in the business.'

'Hush, Pa, don't talk like that. We're not going to lose you.'

But her thoughts had strayed to what might lie behind his words. Was he comparing Nat to Jake, telling her she'd fallen for the wrong Buchanan? He wouldn't be the first to hint at it. Jenny Savage, or Jenny Blake as she was then, had come right out and said it.

'Jake's attractive, but watch him, Blythe. He likes the girls.'

She heard her indignant retort.

'Do you know something about Jake I don't?'

'I know that if I had my chance with the Buchanan's, Nat's the one I'd go for.'

Blythe had smiled.

'And where do you get the idea Nat's interested in me? Good heavens, he thinks I'm part of the Becky Em machinery. One day he's going to come along and try to loosen me up with a squirt of oil and a rub down with a greasy rag.'

Jenny's amusement had lasted briefly. Her voice had dropped.

'You're blind if you can't see the way Nat looks at you.'

But Blythe had dissolved into peals of laughter.

'What an imagination you've got, Jenny. I'm no more than a sister to him. Besides, he pales into insignificance alongside Jake. He's my man. He's romantic, funny, entertaining, adventurous. I think we were destined to be together.'

She shuffled her legs beneath her. How utterly wrong she had been. Hoodwinked by what? The romance of being in love with Murray Bend's most popular bachelor? How odd fate was with Jenny Savage now seeing Nat. Well, good luck to her. Good luck to him. But immediately, her heart slowed. If he married Jenny, married anyone, he would no longer be part of their family. He would have his own for the first time. She shrugged. She had no claim on him, and of course she wanted him to be happy with a woman.

In the background, Nat spoke quietly.

'What pictures do you see in the flames, Blythe?'

'Pardon?' she said.

'You left us for a while there. We were talking about the day we launched the Becky Em. Remember?'

She forced herself back to the present, lightened her voice.

'Remember? Who could forget? Gran had no idea Pa had named it after her, did she? When she sent the el-cheapo bottle of bubbly smashing against it's hull, you whipped off the cover, and there it was, the Becky Em, printed in black block letters along one side. Gran didn't know whether to laugh or cry, so she did both.'

Pa's hand touched her shoulder.

'We all did, Chilli. It's good to hear you laughing again.'

It pleased Nat, too, as he felt her glance moved to him. He took his cue, kept the memories coming.

'And what about the day we double-booked the old tub?'

Already Tom breathed more deeply, sat easier in his chair.

Blythe chimed in, 'What Nat means is the day I double-booked it. I caused all that chaos, but Nat took the blame. And I let him.'

'Who cares? We ran three trips, made extra money.'

On his haunches, Nat placed a large log on the fire, noticed how small she looked, how lifeless her eyes appeared in the light of the flames.

She turned to him and mumbled, 'Thanks, there's a chill in the air.'

He touched her arm.

'You stay by the fire and talk. I'll whip up some omelettes for dinner. You reckon my omelettes are tops, don't you, Tom?'

Blythe forced his hand from her arm and surged to her feet.

'What's so special about yours? He used to enjoy mine, didn't you, Pa?'

'They were very tasty, love, but why not let Nat fix the eggs? You can make the salad. My two best people in the world working together again. Fair enough?'

She shrugged, turned an irritated glance in Nat's direction, but tried to reassure Pa, saying, 'That seems like a good compromise.'

Nat shadow-boxed around Tom's chair, then pretended to punch him in the stomach.

'You old trouble-fixer, you,' he joked as he swung around to Blythe. 'Well, what're you waiting for? Lead me to the kitchen sink, woman.'

There, he put his hands on her shoulders and held her at arm's length.

'I know it's difficult having me around, but if Tom senses the tension, it won't help.'

'Don't you think I know that?'

She avoided his eyes.

'You'll feel better when I move out. I'll go tomorrow morning, no worries. But for now, let's make your first night back as pleasant for him as we can.'

'I'm not going to argue with that.'

She twisted from his hold, went to the fridge and removed a carton of eggs, which she handed to him, as if determined to demonstrate this was her territory. Then in a flurry of activity she located the salad vegetables.

'Has his prognosis changed since we last talked?' she asked.

'No. Unfortunately surgery is out. He's too weak. One night he'll go to bed and not wake up.'

Nat found a bowl and broke in the eggs as he spoke.

'Soon?'

There was a tear in her voice. He heard it above the sounds she made as she found the chopping board, a sharp knife and began rinsing the lettuce leaves.

'The doctors can't give us a time, but he's getting weaker. He only got out of bed today because you were arriving. Talk to the doctor when he calls. He'll fill you in.'

'Look, Nat, if I've seemed edgy . . . '

'Forget it. It's understandable.'

'I want you to know I'm grateful.'

'It's not necessary. I love the old boy. He's been my mentor, a father figure. I owe him and your gran.'

'And you've been generous in repaying him, but I'm here now. Don't feel obliged to us.'

'Come on, Blythe, you know I've never felt obliged.'

He dashed his hand through his hair, feared he was becoming emotional. She smiled then, at least it was an attempt at a smile, but her lips twisted rather than curved.

'Can I offer you some advice for a change?' she said.

'I can't promise to take it.'

'Nat, I've always liked Jenny Savage, and she had rotten luck with her first marriage. If you've got a date with her tonight, you keep it. Girls can be very unforgiving if they're stood up for no good reason.'

'We didn't have a firm arrangement. As a matter of fact, she said she might call over here to say hello. She often calls at night to keep us company.'

Blythe stared at him.

'She does?'

'You don't like her much, do you?'

'For goodness' sake, didn't you hear me say just this minute I like her?'

'Sure you said it, but not very convincingly.'

He tried to catch her attention, but she kept her eyes on her salad making. The shrug of her shoulders signalled her impatience.

'The truth is, things did get a bit cool between us over something she once said about Jake, but she's honest and hard-working and pretty. And I happen to know she's always been sweet on you. Nat, if you love her, don't put things off.'

Her eyes brimmed with tears. At that point, he gave instinct its way, reached out to her, held her close. For minutes she allowed herself to cry in his arms. It had only happened once before, the day she read Jake's suicide note, which was addressed to him. In it, Jake had said, 'Please take care of my Queen of the Fairies.'

If only she would let him.

When she finally looked up, forlorn,

but beautiful in her sorrow, her eyes shimmering pools, her face stained with tears, he forced back his need to soothe her with whispered endearments, to crush her to him. Instead, he tipped her under the chin with his index finger.

'I'm sorry, but I'm all out of handkerchiefs. You took my last one earlier.'

He tried to encourage a smile. She dragged herself from him, found a roll of kitchen paper and ripped off a piece and dabbed at her face.

'I'll be better tomorrow,' she said.

'Of course, you will. Let's get on with dinner. Better to keep things as normal as possible.'

She sighed.

'If only I knew what normal was these days. Anyway, I want to say one more thing, Nat, and please don't take it the wrong way.'

He stopped, the fork he used to beat the eggs poised.

'Shoot.'

'I'm really not up to visitors tonight.

Could you ring Jenny? Go over to her place, by all means, but . . . '

'And leave you on your first night back? No dice. I'll give Jen a bell now.'

He was on his way to retrieve the hand-held set which sat beside Tom, when she added, 'I meant what I said about Jenny. If you love her, marry her. I mean, you're thirty now. It's time you settled down, had children.'

Her mouth curved gently. She was obviously making an effort.

'Yes, grandma, dear. I shall think upon it,' he said, sweeping her a bow

He sounded so easy, but inside, his stomach felt like a diesel engine starved of oil. Jenny was an attractive, uncomplicated and thoughtful woman. She liked the things he liked. She was good company. Now that he thought about it, they could probably make a go of it, and, of course he wanted children, kids on whom he could pour all the love he'd stored up as a child who'd been denied living, caring parents.

The problem was, he didn't love Jenny. He loved someone else, always had, always would. The futility of it scorched through him.

When he returned to the kitchen, Blythe had the salad tossed, the eggs beaten, the pan heating. The cutlery, serviettes and condiments were set out on a tray.

'Step aside,' he jested. 'Tonight I'm wearing the chef's hat.'

She appeared composed.

'Did you speak to Jenny?'

'Yes. I promised I'd bring you over to her place soon as you're up to it.'

'You make me sound like a frail, old lady.'

'She understands, Blythe. She was very fond of . . . '

He gestured with his hands, frustrated, feeling clumsy.

'Does it hurt when I say his name?'

She didn't answer his question. Perhaps she had no answer.

'I know,' she said. 'Jenny has always been fond of the Buchanan boys. Once

I thought she might have been my rival for Jake.'

'Jenny? Rubbish!' He laughed. 'She didn't stand a chance. Jake only had eyes for one person, you.'

This, Nat knew, was a calculated lie. On the steamer trips, Jake attracted the women clients like bees to honey. And sometimes he found the glamorous and sexy ones irresistible.

When Nat chipped him about it, he said once, 'I'm making up for the love I missed out on as a kid. Don't worry, when Blythe and I settle down, I'll give up my philandering ways.'

Nat had glared at him.

'Brother, I won't hurt Chilli, you know that. She's very dear to me. I'm just having fun, sowing the traditional wild oats, before we tie the knot.'

'You'd better not hurt her, mate,' he'd barked back, 'or you'll have me to answer to.'

'And her,' Jake had been quick to add. 'Chilli knows how to look after herself.'

'I don't think you realise how much she loves you.'

'I do. I'm marrying her, aren't I?'

Thank heaven Blythe had been spared the pain of knowing about her fiancé's fondness for other women.

After dinner, Tom insisted on a game of Scrabble.

'Don't agree too readily,' Nat warned Blythe, smiling. 'He's an expert at it. Jenny's taught him words like zymotic. Yes, it's in the dictionary. I looked it up. Jen's very good with words.'

'She's a smart girl, is young Jenny,' Tom added.

Nat began setting up the card table by Pa's chair. Blythe watched, stifling a yawn. Her irritability was on the surge again.

'Can I beg leave?'

'Tom's been longing to show off his skills. Haven't you, old timer?' Nat said.

She took her place at the table. As the only female in the house, Blythe was used to winning, but tonight she was prepared to let Pa take the honours. She soon found under Jenny's tutelage he'd become very sharp.

'Practice,' he explained after she tallied the scores. 'Put it down to young Jenny. And now, Nat, if you'll give me a hand, I'll be off to bed.'

Blythe jumped to her feet, uncoupling his oxygen mask.

'Let me, Pa. That's why I'm here.

He put his hand on her arm.

'You turn down the bed and switch on the blanket, love. Nat'll do the rest.'

'I've already turned on the blanket, Tom.'

Nat handed Pa his walking-stick, stuck out his arm for her grandfather to grasp, and they made their way slowly from the room.

'I'll wheel in the oxygen,' Blythe suggested, feeling left out once more.

'It's OK. I'll come back for it,' Nat said.

'If I'm not needed, I'm off,' she muttered, turning angrily towards her bedroom, but they were chatting and didn't hear her.

Her room looked exactly as it had twelve months ago, as if she'd never left it, except for the spare bed, where she'd placed the large box which held her wedding gown a week before Jake . . . before Jake left. Then, she'd jammed the box under the bed, unable to look at it. Lifting the quilt cover, she reached beneath and eased the box from its hiding place. After placing it on the bed, slowly she raised the lid. The light perfume of soap caught in her nostrils as her fingers drifted over the luxuriant off-white satin, the seed pearls lovingly embroidered along the neck, pointed waist and sleeve lines made years ago by Gran Neilsen.

Gran had made and worn the gown when she married Pa. Blythe had loved its old-fashioned elegance, and at Pa's suggestion had it restored for her own wedding. She raised the bodice from the box, ran the soft, cool material against her cheek. Her heart cried out for Jake, but she had no tears left to stain her face and ease her anguish. The gown fell from trembling fingers to nestle back into its folds into the box, as if it had always been intended to remain there.

'Tom's asking for you.'

Startled, she spun around to find Nat standing at the door.

'He wants to say goodnight. I'm off to bed, too. I was going to ask if you'd like to come for the river trip tomorrow afternoon. You could do the commentary.'

After Pa's semi-retirement, she'd often joined Jake, helping on trips with lively commentary and historical information. A lifetime living at Murray Bend had taught her where every twist and turn, the smallest curves of the river were, the bird life which inhabited its waters and wetlands, nervous parties of kangaroos masking their presence by standing erect like rotted tree trunks. But right now, she was too agitated to give it serious consideration.

'Thanks for your permission to say goodnight to Pa,' she said coldly.

'You looked bushed, and even though he's lost a lot of weight, he leans pretty heavily. You couldn't have managed it, Blythe.'

'In future I will. I'll get a wheelchair for him. I came to look after him and that's what I intend to do.'

'For a week, and then what?'

'I'll stay for as long as he needs me.'

His harsh words had stung her into a rash reply. She had intended to stay only a week. She had commitments, a job back in the city.

'Tom will be choked. I know it's hard, but I'm glad you'll stick around.'

'I'm doing more than sticking around, as you put it. From tomorrow I take over,' she snapped. 'I'm in charge.'

With every sentence, Blythe dug a hole even deeper for herself. Now, she couldn't change her mind and return to the city with any credibility. And she'd made the decision when emotional, tired and irritated. Yet, in her heart she knew she couldn't leave

Pa while he was so ill.

'I thought you'd change your mind about staying. Anyway, I'll be around if and when you need me. I'll be working down in the boatshed repairing engines when I'm not on the river, so I'll call in daily as usual. Tom likes to hear about the boat trips and know the day's takings, and so on. OK?'

'Could I stop you?' she said with a curve of her lips.

'Not a chance. Did you say yes to coming on the Becky Em tomorrow?'

'I'll sleep on it. What time are you going down to the boatshed in the morning?'

'After I get Tom settled.'

'Ahem! Remember? I'm relieving you of your duties, Nurse Buchanan.'

'I usually start around eight-thirty these days.'

'I'll let you know then.'

'And you'll do the commentary?'

It would be good to feel the breeze on her face, see the interest in the eyes of the tourists. But was she ready to plunge back into a life on the river which had dealt her such a crushing blow?

'Who does it these days?' she asked.

'Jenny.'

Who else, she thought, with that odd feeling of resentment which came over her every time Jenny's name cropped up. Slowly the woman had begun to replace her in Pa's and Nat's lives. She set back her shoulders, told herself if she was staying on, she had to face the river, conquer its hold over her and get her life back.

'If Jenny doesn't mind, I think I'd enjoy doing the commentary,' she said.

3

Blythe turned over in bed, groaned and pulled the quilt over her head, trying to hide from the sunshine of a new day filtering through the window. And then with alarm, she remembered. Leaping out of bed, she glared at the clock as she threw on her dressing-gown and finger-combed her hair as she rushed to Pa's bedroom.

Propped up by pillows, he sat in a chair, a breakfast tray across his lap, a radio switched on by the bedside, the curtains opened, and a fire burning in the small grate.

'Chilli, love, did you sleep well?'

His cracked lips managed a smile.

'I did. You see what having you home has done for me?'

She smiled.

'You sound happy. I see Nat's made you very comfortable. Gosh, Pa, I'm ashamed of myself. I intended to be up early to take care of you, and I overslept. Promise you won't sack me.'

'You needed the rest. Nat popped his head in, said you were sleeping. He doesn't mind doing it. Get yourself some brekky and come in and we'll have it together.'

'Don't you move,' she jested. 'I'll be back.'

On her way to the kitchen she listened for sounds of Nat moving around. There were none. In the empty kitchen, grateful she'd been spared the indignity of saying sorry to him again, she found the cereal, poured milk over it, and returned to Pa's room. As she crunched on her cereal, he asked her to switch off the radio. Then he began slowly.

'Chilli, love, I know you're anxious to help me, and that's wonderful because I love you dearly. You're my own flesh and blood. But please, don't shut Nat out.'

'But he's shut me out. I feel he's

taken over my rôle,' she cried.

'Never. No-one can do that. There's something you should know, love. After my heart attack, I couldn't come home unless I had constant care. The doc made arrangements for me to go into a nursing home. And that's where I'd be if it weren't for Nat. He moved back in here, arranged everything, home help, the district nurse, visitors.'

He waved a thin, pale hand.

'But I had no idea. You should have told me. I'd have come home in a flash. I'd never have let you go into a nursing home,' she protested, disappointed that she'd been left out.

'I know, love, but it seemed unfair. You'd been through so much. We decided not to put any more pressure on you.'

'We? You mean you and Nat?'

'We talked it over. In fact, he insisted on moving in, love. He's here in the mornings and evenings, he even pops in at lunchtime to check up on me. He bought one of them phones you carry around in your pocket, and he's got this roster-system of visitors going.'

'Saint Nathaniel,' she muttered.

'What's that?'

Blythe coloured, ashamed that she could feel so bitter towards the man whose only crime had been that he cared for Pa.

'It wasn't important. You love Nat, don't you?'

He nodded.

'Chilli, he's the reason I'm still here. And he knows the river and boats. He's the best brother you could have. I sometimes wish you and him . . . '

He waved a wan hand.

'No matter. Ask him to stay on, please.'

'Of course he stays if it's what you want.'

She touched his hand to reassure him, wishing she could stifle the animosity smouldering in her heart.

'What do you really want, Chilli? That's what's important to me.'

She set down her half-eaten bowl of

cereal and pushed a strand of hair back from her face.

'I don't know, Pa, I just don't know. Sometimes I think I get cross with Nat because he reminds me of Jake. I'm so confused.'

'My poor, little girl. Is it no easier for you?'

'It was, until I came home. But today's another day.'

She stood up and went to stand by the window in the stream of morning sunlight.

'Don't worry, Pa. I'll make it, and so will you. We'll do it together.'

'With Nat's help.'

'With Nat's help,' she repeated and somehow she felt more positive than she had since she first glimpsed the river on her return. 'Today I'm going on the cruise. I've agreed to do the commentary. It's going to be hard, but . . . '

'That's my Chilli. You're made of tough stuff, love. You're a Neilsen.'

He coughed and his breath seemed

to catch in his throat. Blythe hurried across and helped him adjust the oxygen mask.

'You've been talking too much. I think it's time for a snooze.'

Back in the kitchen, Nat had left a note for her. She sighed as she unfolded it and glanced down the schedule and long list of instructions. Nurse Spencer arrived at lunchtime to shower Tom, the doctor called every day at no special time. Mavis Wilson came in at ten to clean and prepare a meal on Tuesdays and Thursdays. A roster of old friends called most afternoons. There were also detailed instructions about Tom's medication, his routine.

However did Nat manage it, and keep the business going, too, and still find time to have a romance with Jenny? She went to the phone and rang her employers in the city. She agreed to return to her position for a few days next week to finish installing a computer programme she'd started. She also rang the agency which handled the lease of her flat and made arrangements to vacate it.

How easily she was closing that fleeting interlude in her life, as easily as if it had no permanence, as if it were a period for marking time.

Nurse Sally Spencer arrived, showered and massaged Tom before resettling him in bed.

'I'd like to get him a wheelchair. I could take him for walks and let him sit in the sun,' Blythe suggested. 'What do you think?'

'He's very weak. Try hiring one for a few days and see how it goes.'

She ran a keen eye over Blythe.

'Don't attempt lifting Tom on your own. Wait until Nat's around to help Tom in and out of the chair. You've lost a lot of weight. Whatever happens, he mustn't have a fall,' she said briskly.

As Blythe began preparing lunch, the phone rang. She answered it quickly in case it disturbed Pa. She recognised Jenny Savage's voice immediately. Blythe talked the niceties of someone who hadn't been around for a while, as she searched her mind for the reason Jenny had rung. Finally, judging it a courtesy call, she short-circuited it.

'Nice to catch up again, Jenny. Do come by any time. The men tell me you're a dab hand at Scrabble.'

Jenny had a little-girl laugh to match her gentle voice.

'They like to flatter me. You know Nat, he only has nice things to say, which brings me to the reason for my call. He asked me to check out what time you'll be down for the boat cruise this afternoon. I'm happy to come over and sit with Tom. Nat doesn't like him being alone for too long.'

Blythe drew in her breath, warned herself to control her temper.

'I didn't intend to leave him alone, Jenny. I'm not that uncaring. In fact I've decided not to leave him today. Can you handle the afternoon tour?'

Jenny hesitated, as if she were considering her words.

'Nat will be disappointed, but I'm

happy to fill in. I love doing the commentary and being Nat's hostess. I was very grateful when he hired me. It's such a pleasant, part-time job.'

'I always enjoyed doing it. We had such fun, Nat, Jake and I.'

Don't let me dissolve into tears, Blythe prayed silently, please don't let it happen.

'You were a wonderful team. I wouldn't presume to . . . '

Blythe switched off. Jenny's self-effacing attitude annoyed her.

'Are you still there, Blythe?'

'Yes.'

'I'd best go. Nat wants me for something. Maybe at the weekend you might fill in. Let me know.'

She managed only a husky, 'Good-bye,' before hanging up and dissolving into tears. As she sat on the kitchen stool dabbing at her eyes, she acknowledged she wept not only for Jake, but for Pa and for Nat. She was losing them, too, she felt, because of her self-indulgent behaviour. She had to stop crying every time someone tested her fragility, and get her mind back into sensible working order. She didn't want to be sidelined and cosseted by Pa's and Nat's pity. Darn it, she wanted their respect, and to be back in their team.

In the bathroom, Blythe splashed cold water over her eyes before looking into the mirror.

'You have to earn your place back,' she told her image. 'You will. That's a promise,' she replied with new-found confidence.

After lunch, she read to Pa. He slept mostly, clutching her hand as if afraid she might desert him while he slept. He wouldn't have done that with Jenny, she reminded herself, and the flame of happiness warmed her.

The musical whistle of the Becky Em sounded. It must be coming around the bend on its home run. Pa opened his eyes. They gleamed.

'Isn't it a wonderful sound, Chilli? A coming home.' Perhaps he read her thoughts, for he added, 'Go out to the front gate and welcome them in, love. Nat will appreciate it. I'll be fine for a few minutes.'

'If you're sure,' she said, but his eyelids were already closed.

She dropped a kiss on his forehead and threw a light jacket over her top, and hurried down the garden. Suddenly, as if her heels had sprouted wings, her feet carried her beyond the front gate, across the bitumen road, over the grassy slope. Shading her eyes with her hand, breathing hard, she saw the boat clear the bend and churn towards the little jetty. The whistle sounded three more times.

It looked so jaunty, a celebration of life with its coloured bunting fluttering in the light breeze, the sound of excited voices echoing across the waters. But when she shifted her focus to the river itself, her lips formed Jake's name and her legs went spongy. She turned away, tormented by the thought that Jake's vigour and dash had disappeared into the shadows of the river. She retreated only a few steps before reminding herself of her earlier promise. She grasped the trunk of a tree, steadied, and forced her arm into the air to wave, her voice to call.

'Hello, Becky Em. Hello-o.'

Her cry drifted across the closing distance. Nat emerged from the wheel-house with two children by his side, doffed his cap and waved back. A cold breeze skipped along her spine, but she gripped the tree still, refusing the urge to shiver. Finally the impulse to flee overcame her and she raced back to the house, slammed the door and leaned against it, panting.

She was preparing dinner, her emotions spent, when Nat's footsteps sounded at the side of the house. Then he called from the back door.

'It's Nat. Am I welcome?'

Determined to lift her mood, she called, 'You're good-looking, so I guess you're allowed.'

As he entered the kitchen, he tipped

his cap to the back of his head and grinned. When he smiled, he was very handsome in a dark, untamed kind of way. The thought rather jolted her, and with it came an odd feeling of shyness. Come on, Blythe, she told herself, and hastily put their relationship back to where it should sit, by reaching up and flipping his peaked cap from his head.

'Have you forgotten? Gentlemen don't wear hats indoors.'

She managed a smile.

'Sorry,' he said. 'It's not having you around. Occasionally the gentleman in me goes absent without leave.'

She laughed, the awkwardness gone.

'The gentleman in you? It's always absent without leave as far as I'm concerned. And, by the way, I'll make an appointment tomorrow for you to have your hair cut. I'll come with you. I need a trim myself.'

'Hey, there's no need. I bought a do-it-yourself kit. I look after Tom's hair, too. Would you care to make an appointment with Captain Buchanan for a trim, little lady?'

'Not on your life. You're going to a proper hairdresser. Pa's got an excuse, you haven't. I'm surprised Jenny hasn't insisted before this.'

She flicked his cap back to him. He caught it expertly in one hand.

'Jenny has no say. She knows better than to try and take over your rôle.'

He reached for the kettle as she stepped between him and the bench.

'Don't you dare touch anything until you've washed up. It amazes me the whole house isn't stained with engine oil without a woman around.'

Smiling to herself, she filled the kettle and turned on the switch.

'And what do you mean, my rôle? I think you're having a piece of me, Captain Buchanan.'

'Could be.'

'Go clean up. I'll make the tea.'

'I'll pop in and see Tom first. Is he OK?'

'After you've cleaned up.'

'You're back in form.'

'If you mean I'm running the household, you're spot on. Actually, I'm wondering if we could get Tom up for dinner.'

'We'll ask him, eh? Did you do anything about a wheelchair? It was a good idea.'

'Nurse Spencer suggested I hire one first to see how he goes. I've been in touch with the pharmacy and ordered it. She also thinks you should be around to get him in and out of it.'

'A very sensible woman, Sally Spencer.'

He turned on his way out, as if it were an after-thought, and with the old concern back in his dark eyes, asked, 'You are OK with that, aren't you?'

'Yes. From now on, promise, I'm going to be easier to get along with.'

'Smile when you say that.'

His teeth looked very white and strong against his tanned complexion. Again the feeling of shyness flickered over her. It had to be that he reminded her of Jake. What else could it be? She wiped her brow and pushed on with dinner preparations.

When Nat returned, he'd changed into jeans and a dark T-shirt. The phrase, seriously good-looking, flashed through her mind. The feeling of uneasiness being alone with him persisted. She forced conversation.

'Sorry I slept in this morning, and I hope you didn't pack your things. Pa wants you to stay on at the house.'

He came across and stood close to her. His damp hair gleamed and curled across his broad forehead, over the neck of his T-shirt.

'And you? What do you want?'

'You're demanding your pound of flesh, aren't you? You want me to beg you to stay,' she suggested.

'I'd like you to ask, not beg,' he said gruffly.

She nodded.

'Of course, I'm asking you, on one condition. You and I go to the hairdresser in the next day or two.'

Impulsively, she reached up and

ruffled his hair with her hand. As he smiled down at her, her heart quickened.

'You're on. See if you can get a late appointment.'

Unsure, she moved the conversation on.

'How was Pa when you went in? Would he like to get up?'

'Not tonight. He's pretty beat. I guess having his lovely nurse around all day has upped his temperature.'

She kept on peeling the potatoes, secretly pleased.

'But Jenny wasn't here today.'

'You know I mean you.'

'You hand out compliments so rarely.'

'Yeah? I always thought you were streets ahead of the other girls around here. I don't have to say it. You know it. If it hadn't been for . . . oh, forget it.'

He held up his hands. Indecision, or was it uncertainty, or both, darkened his eyes. The potato slipped from Blythe's grasp. She grabbed it back.

The room grew very still, very small. She felt . . . she felt . . . she didn't know how she felt. Flattered? Surprised? Amazed? Streets ahead of the other girls around here, he'd said. Including Jenny?

Leave it, she warned herself. Your emotions can't handle anything more at the moment. She distanced herself from his gaze.

'We're having grilled steak for dinner. Does that suit?' she asked quietly.

'Excellent. I had this dreadful foreboding that Sydney might turn you into a pasta freak. I'll set the table.'

He reached for the cloth and flung it across the table, then noisily pulled open the cutlery drawer. She suspected the silence between them made him uncomfortable, too.

'There'll be plenty of pasta while I'm in charge, but I noticed the steak in the fridge and thought I'd better use it before it went mouldy,' she teased to ease the strain.

'You know, we blokes managed very

well for twelve months while you were gone.'

She dared to look up. He was grinning. Like Jake, he had a wonderful smile. How come she'd only started to notice?

Again, silence invaded the room, unnerving her, pushing her to find a quick rejoinder.

'But I'm back, and I'll have you back in shape in no time.'

She nicked herself with the potato peeler. She sucked her finger and told herself to concentrate on what she was doing.

'If you're expecting me to salute and say, 'aye, aye', I remind you I'm the one who wears the captain's hat around here.'

His laugh sounded forced. He followed quickly with, 'Say, Blythe, why don't we eat in Tom's room?'

Relief flooded through her. The thought of dining across the table from him in the small kitchen had stirred butterflies to frantic flight in her stomach.

'What a good idea. Can you set things up in there?'

'Sure.'

He wrapped up the cloth and cutlery in one efficient swoop and left. Blythe mopped her brow. They'd have to make other arrangements about job-sharing in the kitchen until she got over this sudden fixation about Nat. Going hot and cold, getting goose bumps because of him only made sense if she blamed it on his likeness to Jake. But he didn't have Jake's luminous blue eyes. His were warm, darker than dark.

They played only one game of Scrabble before Tom asked to be settled for the night. The sensible thing would have been to retire then, but Blythe felt chilly. Nat must have noticed her slight shiver.

'I'll stoke the fire in the sitting room. You can't go to bed cold,' he said.

She followed him into the room, watched his strong arms flex as he threw several logs on to the fire before dropping into a winged chair, stretching his long legs. As usual she sat on the floor, her back against Pa's chair, her legs curled under her. She leaned towards the fire, held out her hands and gazed into the leaping flames. She didn't intend to linger, just to warm up.

'I've been intending to ask you,' Nat began. 'I hope it's not too soon.'

Her stomach muscles tightened.

'Too soon for what?'

'Back at our place, I've left Jake's room pretty much as it was. Would you like to go through his things, perhaps keep some of them? Or would you prefer to wait a bit?'

Though Nat consistently insisted there was nothing in Jake's possessions to help explain his suicide, Blythe had often thought Jake must have left behind something, some clue. It could be in his room, but until now, she'd lacked the courage to even visit the house he shared with Nat. If she could steel herself to go through his things, maybe . . .

'Not yet,' she replied in little more

than a whisper, 'but sometime soon.'

'I'm not pushing you. Go when you're ready. Have you still got a key to the place?'

'I think so.'

'Would it help if I came with you?'

'Thanks, Nat, but it's something I have to do alone.'

His presence would inhibit her search. If there was something in Jake's room to help her understand, she would find it.

'I might go over one night while you're here with Pa.'

'If you're alone, I'd sooner you go during the day while one of Tom's mates is visiting.'

Nat knew Blythe wouldn't find anything to give away Jake's penchant for women, for he had removed photographs, magazines, his brother's scribbled phone numbers in an out-of-date diary. After the police inspected them, dismissed them as unhelpful, he'd locked them away in his desk.

'Perhaps in a week or two.'

Her voice sounded shaky and he thought she shivered, and wished he hadn't mentioned it. She spoke on, her tone recovering as she changed the subject.

'By the way, I promised to go back to the city for a few days next week to finish a computer programme I started, and to clean out my flat. While I'm gone, can you suggest someone to come in for a few hours each day? I'd pay them.'

'Ask Jenny. She won't mind.'

'Not Jenny.'

Blythe straightened her back against the chair.

'I mean, it's unfair to expect her to drop everything to suit me.'

'Then persuade yourself she's doing it for me and Tom.'

'I already know that, but we can't impose on her all the time. It's not as if she's a member of the family.'

She turned to face him, her chin jutted with determination. He kept the impatience from his voice.

'I don't understand this. What's she done to upset you?'

Blythe shrugged. What could she say that made any sense? That Jenny made her feel uneasy? That she couldn't bear to lose his and her pa's affection especially after Jake?

'Nothing. I just don't think it's fair to keep on asking her to do things for us. She has a life of her own. If we offered to pay her . . . '

He laughed.

'You can't be serious. She'd be very offended. I don't think you realise how much she's done for your pa and how fond he's grown of her.'

'And of you?' she chipped in.

'Yeah. We're good mates. We help one another out. If she needs repairs done around her place, lawns mown, she asks me. Look, if you must give her something, bring her back a gift from the city.'

'What do you suggest? Flowers, chocolates, something sensual?' Blythe snapped.

'Surely you're not jealous of Jenny!' Nat snapped. 'She's been so caring and helpful these last few months. I don't know how we'd have managed. I can't believe your sarcasm. It's downright ungrateful of you, Blythe.'

He turned away.

'But you're running the show now. If Jenny makes you uncomfortable, and heaven knows why she should, ask Sally Spencer to arrange something. I'm off. I hope you'll get out of bed on the right side in the morning. Goodnight!'

She hurried to her feet.

'Oh, no, I've done it again,' she cried out. 'Forgive me, Nat. I'm sorry, really I am. Of course I'll ask Jenny. I know how much you care for her.'

'This isn't about me, it's about how fond she is of Tom. And I'm getting fed-up with hearing you say sorry. Next time, I hope you mean it.'

Nat stalked off, but turned when she said plaintively, 'I know I'm a pain. It's taking time for me to ease my way back. Nothing seems the same since Jake

. . . since Jake left us.'

He crossed towards her, holding her close.

'My suggestion that you go through Jake's room brought this on, didn't it? It was thoughtless of me.'

He tilted her chin with his finger.

'Forget what I said. There's no need for you to go until you're ready.'

Blythe nodded, accepting his explanation, though it was not the mention of Jake which had triggered her display of petulance. It was the realisation that she felt a bit jealous of Nat's and Pa's affection for Jenny. Losing Jake had left Blythe feeling terribly insecure, and if she wasn't careful that insecurity might turn Nat away from her, too. Life without his friendship would be intolerable.

Tomorrow she would start behaving with maturity.

4

Blythe insisted Nat visit the hairdresser, so they went together, laughing at the bounty of black hair around the floor of the chair as the hairdresser's scissors assaulted his unruly mop.

'Very smart,' she told him afterwards, smiling.

'My neck's cold,' he grumbled.

'But you weigh much lighter.'

'Coffee?' he suggested.

They called into a once-favoured coffee shop, ordered cappuccino and two decadent chocolate éclairs. As they licked their fingers like children, he leaned across and with the pad of his finger removed a crumb from the corner of her mouth. It was the kind of thing Jake might have done. Her heart's steady beat went astray.

The longer she spent alone with Nat, the more she saw how alike he and his brother were, not in personality, but in voice inflection, phrases, silhouette, especially now Nat had his hair short. There were moments, and today, right now, in this light-hearted mood, was one of them, when she really felt the presence of Jake.

As they strolled up the mall, discussing the changes to the shops, she'd glance up, see a gesture of his hands, a tilt of his head, which left her unnerved until her appraisal reached his eyes. Nat didn't have Jake's gleaming blue eyes. That brought her back to reality. But being with Nat was a comfortable, secure reality, one she enjoyed.

That night, Blythe asked, 'Would it be all right to come on the Becky Em over the weekend? Pa's been urging me to take a trip. I think I'm up to it.'

'Great. We've got a full complement of passengers on Sunday. Come on the afternoon trip. There'll be lots to do. You and Jenny can share the commentary and look after the souvenir shop. I don't think you've seen Jen since you arrived back, have you?'

Blythe still experienced a tinge of envy, or was it insecurity, when Nat mentioned Jenny.

'I had thought Jenny might sit with Pa.'

'No need. We'll organise someone. If there's one thing this town boasts, besides the tourists, it's retired men who love to talk about the good, old days.'

She smiled, remembering the group of elderly men who'd been sitting on a seat in the mall, soaking up the last of the sun.

'I've noticed. It'll be good to finally catch up with Jenny, too.'

She meant it. She'd adopted an uncharitable attitude to Jenny, and she had to turn it around.

On Sunday morning, a weak winter sun broke through the clouds after a frosty start. At unexpected moments Blythe felt a nervous flutter of her heart. Could she really go on board the

Becky Em, recapture the magical moments they'd once had as a threesome? Of course not, Jake would be missing. They were only two now. But she paused as that wasn't right. There was Jenny. She tossed her shoulders back. It was up to her to make it work.

After lunch, she changed into navy slacks, her monogrammed white shirt which still hung in her wardrobe, draped the white scarf, overprinted with yellow rope and navy anchors, around her neck and plumped up her hair.

'Captain Neilsen,' she called, 'prepare yourself. I'm coming in for your inspection.'

Then she hurried into his room and twirled in front of him. Pa laughed.

'You approve, Captain Neilsen?' she asked happily.

'You seem more relaxed these days, and I'm glad you've put on a bit of weight since you came home.'

'Are you telling me the pants are baggy or tight?'

She patted the waist of her trousers.

'They're fine. Now run along. Don't be late on your first day back, and enjoy yourself.'

She kissed him.

'I wish you were coming, too. Soon you'll be strong enough to take a trip in your wheelchair. You're looking much better.'

'It's your influence, love.'

She smiled.

'What time is your friend coming?'

'Bill'll be here any time. Now toodle-oo.'

Slipping her purse over her shoulder, she picked up her file of commentary notes, and hesitated, unwilling to leave Pa alone. As if to ease her conscience, a knock sounded on the back door. She breathed more freely, and trotted off to let Bill in. But Jenny stood on the doorstep. She wore the uniform of the Becky Em, too. Her once-chubby face had thinned, her long hair had been trimmed, shaped and darkened. She looked beautiful. Did being in love with

Nat give her this natural but appealing beauty?

'Jenny, how nice to see you. I thought we were to meet on board.'

'I decided you'd be more comfortable doing the commentary on your own. I thought I'd use the break to pop in and say hello to Tom. I haven't seen him since you arrived home.'

'I hope I haven't kept you away.'

Jenny's smile didn't reach her eyes. She changed the subject.

'I hear you're good at Scrabble.'

'Not as good as you, apparently. Come in. Pa will be pleased to see you. Bill is coming around to stay with him, so don't feel you have to hang around for ever.'

'Good. We might have a threesome of cards.'

Jenny sounded a little too enthusiastic, as if she were trying to impress everyone.

'You'll have to excuse me if I hurry away. By the way, it was Nat's suggestion that I share the commentary with you today. Naturally I thought he'd cleared it with you. I hope you don't feel as if I'm trying to take your job away from you, Jenny.'

'Of course not. I realise you only have to say the word and you're back in charge. In Nat's eyes, when you're around, I'm always second in line.'

Her voice had an edge to it.

'You're mistaken, Jenny. Nat's very grateful for the support and back-up you give him and Tom, and so am I.'

'Grateful?' Jenny's question had a mocking ring to it.

The word lingered in Blythe's mind as she stepped briskly down to the Becky Em. Jenny obviously wanted more from Nat than he had as yet offered, but it was clear she hadn't given up hope of getting him. It was unfair and immature of her to want to hold on to Nat, to feel even vaguely jealous of the time and attention he gave to Jenny.

Nat had the chance of a marriage and children with Jenny. There was only one way to put an end to the uncomfortable situation that had developed between her and Jenny. Nat had to make a decision about Jenny. She'd talk to him tonight. Her heart missed a beat. She quickly put it down to the anticipation of going on board the Becky Em for the first time in almost a year.

The river boat swayed gently at anchor. The sunlight captured the freshly-painted blue trim around the hull, the grating over the paddle wheel. The bright bunting and the canvas of the picnic chairs on the upper deck shimmied in the gentle breeze, luring the passengers to its side. Jenny was forgotten. The sound of the whistle piping into the majestic stillness, the sight of Nat waiting for her at the walkway on to the boat, all filled her with a strange, stirring emotion.

He raised his arm and waved. She lengthened her stride, almost ran. He shoved his cap back on his head, his dark eyes inviting. He reached out his hand to her. She accepted it, walked the gently-swaying plank between jetty and boat, and stepped on to the deck. A sense of happiness, of coming home, brought tears to her eyes.

'Welcome back.'

Nat placed his arm around her shoulders.

'Are you OK with everything?'

'It's so good to be here. You've got the boat looking fantastic, Nat. Freshly painted. It's great. I should have come down sooner. Has anything in the programme changed? I hope I can do things well for you.'

She shot the questions at him.

'Hey, slow down. Nothing much has altered, but knowing you, you'll soon pick up any changes. You're a natural at this job. Would you like to start by collecting the tickets as the passengers come on?'

'I've love to, but first I'd better test the mike, and get the urns filled. You see,' she said with a smile, 'I haven't forgotten.'

As she set off, he reached out and gripped her arm.

'Not necessary. Jenny did that before she left. I pushed the switches just now.'

For a moment she hesitated, her happy mood clouded. Just one more example of how easily she had been replaced by Jenny, but today nothing, not even her confused feelings about Jenny, would spoil her day.

'Good. Anything else I need to know?'

'Today, I want you to relax and enjoy yourself,' Nat replied.

'I intend to, but let me know if I need to do a retraining course.'

She strolled across to the boat's point of entry, and removed the rope barrier so the patrons could come on board. Very little had changed. Blythe noticed how the older children gravitated to the rails, where they stood hoping the water would wash up and spray them, where they faced into the wind, their hair streaming behind them. The wheel-house was another popular spot. There

Nat allowed them to handle the wheel occasionally. Most of the elderly chose to sit in the comfort of the glassed-in lower deck.

The whistle sounded, once, twice, three times, and the boat laboured out into the deep channel, unhurried, steady. That was life on the river. This was her heritage, she thought. Blythe loved the sounds of children, the chatter of the throng, the questions.

'How old is the Becky Em?' they asked again today.

'It was built at Goolwa, at the mouth of the Murray, in the late eighteen hundreds and traded along the river for many years. Like most other paddle-steamers, it was abandoned when road and rail travel replaced the river,' she answered.

Then her voice filled with pride.

'My grandfather always knew this particular steamer would have a second life. He had plans for it as soon as he spotted it rotting by the river bank. But he had to wait until retirement to restore it to working condition. Later the steam engine was replaced with a diesel. Of course, he couldn't have done it without Captain Nat. My grandfather had the dream, Captain Nat had the know-how.'

She glanced across at Nat and smiled. He tipped his cap, smiled broadly, in acknowledgement of her praise, and the clapping which came from the tourists. Lazily, the Becky Em made its way upstream, until they reached their destination, where Captain Nat invited a couple of children who had shown particular interest to sound the whistle. It alerted Curley, an old river man who now lived in a shack by the water, that the boat had arrived.

Nat employed Curley to prepare afternoon tea, and to chat to the passengers about the history of the river. The aroma of cooking filled the air. The fire, over which hung a big black kettle and a billycan, sent sparks drifting into the breeze. Water birds made a quick retreat, calling their families in clear, musical notes. Curley, with a flair for showmanship, swung the billycan containing boiling water and tea leaves in a circular motion to demonstrate how proper bush tea was made. He served it in enamel mugs with slices of warm bread made in the warm ashes, dripping with butter. Blythe handed out biscuits and soft drinks for the children.

When the whistle sounded three more times, the passengers clamoured aboard and the Becky Em turned for home. Blythe identified a group of pelicans sitting on the limb of a partly-submerged tree. Then she spotted a pair of rather rare Australian cranes elegantly wheeling and fluttering.

'Have your cameras ready in case they settle,' she suggested.

Towards the end of the trip, with her duties almost over. Blythe went out to the sundeck, where she stood, the breeze in her face, leaning against the rail. An attractive, young woman approached her, golden hair, high cheekbones, sleek in tight jeans and a body-hugging black sleeveless top, a camera in hand.

'Hello, I'm Sarah,' she said. 'I enjoyed your commentary. I hope I've managed to take a few good photos.'

'Have you enjoyed the day?'

'I always do. It's a great trip. I miss the river.'

'Then you're not living here now?'

'I'm in Melbourne. Jake was helping run things the last time I came on board. Such a looker, and personality plus. You can imagine how chuffed I was when he invited me out to dinner.'

Her voice faltered.

'I was devastated when I heard the news. I can't believe he killed himself.'

'Of course he didn't,' Blythe cried, before putting her hand to her mouth to stifle another outburst. 'I'm sorry,' she murmured. 'I must get back downstairs. I've got work to finish before we berth.'

Swinging away from the woman, she stumbled down the stairs and into the alcove at the back of the souvenir shop. There she tried to regain her composure. As she stemmed the flow of tears with a handful of tissues, it registered that the woman called Sarah claimed Jake had taken her out to dinner. She needed to talk to her again, to question her about her relationship with Jake, and to discover if she knew anything that might help her to understand. Seizing up sunglasses to hide her swollen eyes, she raced back upstairs, hoping she might catch Sarah before she left the boat, but apparently she had already departed. The knot in her stomach twisted. Perhaps Nat knew this Sarah.

Nat stayed on to attend to the maintenance of the boat. Blythe walked home slowly. Unready to be questioned about her day, or to make light conversation, it relieved her to find Jenny had left, and Pa was asleep. Pa's visitor, Bill, had also fallen asleep in a chair beside his bed. It must have been a lively conversation, she thought, vaguely amused, and then realised how weary she felt herself. The fresh air out there on the river, the sunshine, the emotion of her meeting with this Sarah had tired her. She sat in Tom's ample sitting room chair, stretched out, and fell into a restless sleep.

She dreamed of a shapely blonde woman, with a cruel laugh, who kept shouting something to her through scarlet lips. But the breeze swept the words away, and when she moved closer to hear them, the woman materialised in another location on the boat's deck. Blythe woke sweating. Nat was calling her name. She glanced at her watch. It was almost six o'clock. He laughed at her as he entered.

'Sleeping on the job, eh?'

She hurried to her feet.

'I dozed off for a minute or two, no more.'

'No need to apologise. I've asked Bill to stay on for dinner. Poor old blighter cooks for himself most nights.'

'You might have consulted the cook.'

She stretched her limbs, yawned, feeling out of sorts.

'I noticed you'd prepared a casserole. It looked as if it would go four ways with a few extra veg. I'll fix them. Tom and Bill are playing poker for matchsticks at the moment. I'll leave you to entertain the troops.'

Blythe looked in on the older men, exchanged a few words and then went into the kitchen.

'They're happy. I'll give you a hand. I want to talk to you, anyway,' she said to Nat.

As they shared the preparations, she said in as natural a voice as possible, 'Has it ever occurred to you how attractive Jenny has grown?'

'I hadn't noticed,' he said absently.

'You know she regards me as a rival for your affections. She as much as admitted it. It's laughable, isn't it?'

'Laughable indeed.'

'Yes. You and me.'

She tilted her head to reinforce her statement, yet uncertainty clouded her thoughts so that she had no idea how she really felt.

Nat didn't think he'd been super-subtle about his feelings. Blythe must be very blind. Of course she wasn't a rival with Jenny for his affections. Blythe had no rivals. She'd captured and held his heart at least a decade ago, but the victory had gone to Jake, and because her happiness meant so much to him, he'd made it his mission to ensure that Jake did the right thing by her.

But he'd failed her.

After his brother's death, in rare buoyant moments, he allowed himself to hope that one day she might fall for him. But because of her vulnerability, he expected if it were to happen, it would take time. Sometimes such as now, he lied to her, pretended.

'You and me? I hope you told Jenny she's got a sci-fi imagination,' he said, wondering why her eyes shimmered, and she looked away hurriedly.

'I've tried to reassure her, but there's this barrier between us, stopping us from being good friends the way we used to be. She's in love with you, Nat, I'm sure of it. And I can't believe you don't know it. If you love her, tell her. If you don't, you risk losing her. She's not going to hang around for ever.'

Her voice wasn't very convincing. He sighed, put down the knife he was using to slice the potatoes and placed his hands on her shoulders.

'Blythe, she's a good friend. Don't try to turn it into something that isn't there.'

'You mightn't realise it, Nat, or intended it, but you've built up her expectations. And sometimes I wonder if my coming back has spoiled things for the two of you.'

'You coming back is only good news for all of us.'

'Nat, you're not listening. Pa thinks you and Jenny are an item. He must have picked up vibes.'

'Tom knows that I want a family. A girl only has to smile at me and he's got me married to her.'

'He's watched you and Jenny. She'd make a wonderful wife and mother. If you're stringing her along . . . '

'Would I do that to a woman?' he chipped in, trying to keep things light.

This wasn't a conversation he wanted to have. In truth, he'd suspected Jenny's feelings towards him were more than friendly, and maybe he should be discouraging her, but somehow the relationship drifted on. If it got out of control . . .

'I'll speak to her, Dr Feelgood. Satisfied?'

'It depends what you say. At least convince her you and I are just good friends as they say in the classics.'

She looked up and smiled at him. He loved her dark, warm eyes, especially when they met his with this special intimacy they had. If it could go on, if he could hold her, feel her body against his, stroke her hair, taste her lips, tell her he loved her. But that was impossible while love for Jake lingered in her heart. It was time to escape, where the air wasn't fragrant with her perfume, tense with his feelings.

'I'll pop in and get the men settled by the fire. I'll be back soon.'

He moved towards the door, but Blythe had one more question.

'Nat,' she began slowly, casually, she hoped, 'before you go, I've been meaning to ask if you know anyone called Sarah.'

He swung around, stared at her with, was it surprise, suspicion, anger?

'Several Sarahs, actually. What age are we looking at here?'

'Any age.'

She weaved the lie as she went.

'It's just that I remember Jake mentioning a Sarah. It's not a name I know. I thought if he was fond of this person, I'd like to talk to her.'

Nat flopped into a nearby chair, dashing his hand through his hair.

'Surely Jake told you at one time or another that our birth mother's name was Sarah.'

Blythe drew in her breath.

'Your mother!'

She shook her head and her mind took flight into regions 'way beyond those which included the young woman she'd met on the boat.

'I didn't know, Nat. What if Jake had tracked her down? What if that had something to do with . . . '

'You're grasping at straws, Blythe,' he interrupted. 'Jake hated his mother for giving him up. He'd never have searched for that cold-hearted creature.'

She went to his side and sat on the arm of his chair.

'Supposing she located him, somehow? He might have been receptive. He might have wanted to see her and tell her what he really thought.'

'You're asking all these questions, Blythe, digging up the past simply because someone mentioned the name Sarah? Leave it, Blythe. It's a common enough name, particularly these days. I'll bet you know a few Sarahs yourself. And anyway, it's none of your business.'

He surged to his feet, jolted her, unbalanced her. She reached out to him to steady herself, but he avoided her, leaving her bewildered by his anger. He would come back, she assured herself, apologise, make his peace, as he always did.

This time, however, she was mistaken.

5

I think I'm up to going through Jake's things now,' Blythe said to Nat a few nights later. 'Is tomorrow too soon?'

He had his head buried in a magazine. He had been distant towards her since she'd reawakened the memories of his mother, Sarah. If only she'd known, she'd never have mentioned the name Sarah in his presence. He looked up abruptly, as if surprised.

'Are you sure you're ready?' he asked coolly.

'No, but it's something I have to try to do. I can't go on avoiding things.'

'My offer to come with you still holds.'

She shook her head, the needle of her tapestry work poised.

'I prefer to go alone so I can take my time. I'll probably weep buckets.'

She'd intended to sound casual, but

her lower lip dropped as she fought back the tears. Nat tossed his magazine aside.

'Don't sit on my needlework,' she said though tear-glazed eyes as he kneeled by her chair. 'You might get pricked and sleep for one hundred years.'

He stood up, put his arm about her shoulders, and as his strong, lean fingers indented the soft flesh of her forearm, it sent a feeling of tranquillity through her.

'And you wouldn't even miss me.'

He handed her his handkerchief.

'I can't imagine not having you around, Nat. When I was in Sydney, sometimes I'd feel down. I'd look around, searching for something. I used to think it was for Jake, but I know now, I was searching for you. You've always been there for me,' she murmured. 'I loved Jake, but it's you I always turn to when I need strength. Thanks for always being there for me.'

'That's why gutsy sisters have big brothers.'

He crushed her more closely to him and then releasing her, resumed his place in the chair.

'You've got a key to the old place, haven't you?'

'Yes.'

She nodded, feeling the emptiness beside her, a confusion about why she wished he still held her, afraid of the uncertainty which sometimes swept her up, when she forgot her love for Nat was the brotherly kind.

Next day, Blythe pulled her car into the driveway of the familiar, old Buchanan home. Taking a deep breath, she turned off the engine, determined to stay focused, in control of her emotions. She'd come in search of answers, not to weep and dream.

Nat had bought the house on the edge of a caravan park overlooking the river. Inexpensive because of its poor condition, Nat saw its potential immediately. Its beauty, he explained to the family, who as one advised against its purchase, lay in its unspoiled, natural setting with its river views. It could be restored to its original condition, and he'd proved his point.

As she made her way to its river frontage, the sun came out, flooding her with memories of long summer days when she and Jake had stretched out under the shady trees after swimming. Jake had suspended an old tyre from a rope looped across one of the overhanging boughs. It still hung there. He used to swing out on it and drop into the water. She loved watching his bronzed, athletic figure, his laughter, the splash as he hit the river.

'Don't ever lose the little boy in you,' she used to say. 'It's so endearing.'

He'd kiss her lips briefly.

'Yes, Gran.'

The sound of his voice came to her in the silence of the bush. Forcing herself on, she blinked away her tears and inserted the key in the front door. Inside, she fingered away the remnants of tears, set back her shoulders and reminded herself of her mission. Busying herself, she flung open the blinds and pushed up several windows. The shafted light picked up dust on furniture, and cobwebs laced around the light fittings, across the ceiling beams. In the unnerving silence, memories crowded in on her.

Nat had offered the house to her and Jake once they married, but Jake had said, 'Thanks, mate, but we're going to live on our boat, aren't we, sweetheart?'

They hadn't discussed the idea together. It hadn't figured in her plans, but Jake was like that, making spur-of-the-moment statements. He'd soon work out they were never going to afford the luxury boat they'd blue-printed in their minds by the time they married. But so what? She loved his romanticism. Wasn't that the difference between a marriage and a happy marriage? She'd laughed.

'We certainly are, Nat. Besides, you love this house. We couldn't allow you to give it up. But thanks for being so generous.'

Blythe pushed herself into the passage leading to Jake's bedroom. Her heels made an uneasy sound on the polished boards, echoing through the abandoned house. She felt achingly alone. Jake's door stood open. The room looked exactly as it always had, except he wasn't lolling on the bed, propped up on one arm, reading a magazine. His luminous blue eyes didn't look up, sparkle a greeting to her. Jake was no longer here.

The photograph of her, perched on the rail of the Becky Em wearing Jake's peaked cap at a rakish angle, smiling, giving the thumbs up sign, stood on the bedside table.

'It's not very feminine,' she'd protested when he had it enlarged and framed.

'It's fun,' he'd said. 'It's how I think of you.'

Perhaps she should have protested, but as usual, his grin, the kiss which accompanied his statement easily won her over. Blythe lifted the picture now, the lamp, the lace cloth. Nothing was hidden or mislaid there. She opened the drawers and went through them one by one, removing them, sending her fingers probing into the corners. She had no idea what she looked for, but hoped something might catch her attention, spark her memory.

Before replacing the drawers, she put aside Jake's leather wallet, a mahogany box in which he kept a watch, the gold tie clip and cuff links with the Becky Em logo. Tom had given them to him on his twenty-first birthday. These were his personal things, things to take away, to touch, to stroke, to belong, to keep the memory alive.

Next she upended the mattress, searching every crease in the bed clothes, inside the pillowcases. She turned over the floor rugs, sneezing as a puff of dust reached her nostrils. Nothing significant there. The wardrobe was her last hope. One by one she went through the pockets of his jackets, trousers, shirts. His fragrance reached out to her. Crazily, she almost threw her arms around his steamer shirt. Always tears tarried behind her eyes, impatient, threatening, but she held them off. Blurred vision, emotional turmoil must not hamper her search. If, hidden away, there was some clue to help her understand, she had to find it but she found nothing — no letters, no photos, nothing.

Doggedly, she made one final effort, and using the inside of the wardrobe as the rung of a ladder, she stretched up and felt along the top of the old closet. Aha! It had a recess for storage. An ideal hiding place. She held her breath as her hands searched the space and finally, she breathed out. She'd found something. Her fingers gripped a handle. She dragged at it. In the flurry, Jake's Becky Em peaked cap came, too. It floated to the floor, but in her hand, she held a cheap, old suitcase.

After placing the cap on the bedside

table with the other things she intended to take away, with heady anticipation she examined the case. It was locked, of course, and no key. Her fingers trembled as she attempted to force open the rusted lock. It didn't budge. She raced out to the garage, returned with a screw driver and levered it into the lock. Still it refused to free up. Blythe hurled the case to the floor.

'Please, Jake, speak to me. Tell me why. Where are you? I know the river didn't have the power to take you. You tamed it years ago.'

Flopping on to the bed, she buried herself into its folds, into what should have been Jake's arms, and wept, and that was where Nat found her, curled up, shivering, clutching something to her breast. He held her to him. He wished so much, and not for the first time, that it had been him and not Jake who had died. He wished he had Jake's charm, Jake's knock-about ways, his zest for the good life. He could have been a substitute, offered Blythe something to soothe her aching heart, second-best, but something.

She clung to him until her sobbing stopped. When she turned her tear-stained face up to him, it tore at his heart. Yet he could do nothing to ease her pain.

'You'll have to give this one back. I'm fast running out of handkerchiefs,' he said, attempting a smile, reaching into his pocket, to deliver one with a quick, jerky movement, afraid to let her go.

'Oh, Nat, it's been awful, and I can't get that case opened.'

He followed her gaze to the old case resting against the wall. She put down Jake's wallet, scrubbed away at her face and snuffled into the handkerchief like a child.

'Where did you find it?' Nat asked, his stomach tightening.

He remembered it, but hadn't seen it in years. Suppose Jake had things in it he didn't want Blythe to see?

'It was on top of the wardrobe. But I

couldn't open it. The lock's rusted.'

'I'll soon fix that.'

He put her away from him, and placing himself between her and the case to obstruct her view, he jerked it ajar. The contents stared back at him. Breathing more easily, he wondered vaguely if he should prepare Blythe. But before he could decide, she was by his side, gazing into the case's contents. A soft toy rabbit and a few old photographs stared back at them. Blythe gasped.

'What are they? Were they Jake's?'

'Yes,' Nat nodded. 'They're the things he coveted as a child, remnants of his life before we were fostered. I'd forgotten all about them. While he was growing up, and especially after he'd been given a belting in one of those foster homes, he used to look at the photos and ask me why his real mother gave him away. I was eight when it happened, but he was only two. Poor little sod.'

She picked up the creased pictures

and ran her finger over them.

'He was such a beautiful little boy. How could anyone have given him away?'

Rejected children only felt rage, could offer only an emotional response to a question like that. Nat stifled his rage with an attempt at being practical.

'Perhaps because they didn't want children in the first place. Perhaps because they weren't capable of looking after children. Who knows? Would you like to keep the pictures and the rabbit?'

He replaced them in the case.

'Jake would want you to have them.'

'If you're prepared to part with them.'

She picked up the wallet and the mahogany box.

'I'd like to have these, too, if you're OK with that.'

He nodded.

'There are also his sporting trophies through in the living room. Do you want them?'

'Perhaps.'

She seemed calmer.

'I'll go through them later.'

'OK, then, ready to go home?'

She left the case for him, and tucking it under his arm, he followed her from the room. Outside, still ahead of him, Blythe walked straight-backed, her shoulders stiff, as if she might crumble to the ground if she relaxed.

'I rowed across in the canoe,' he said. 'I'll drive you home, if you like.'

Suddenly she turned back, wild-eyed. Startled, he watched her race past him back to the house, crying out, 'I forgot! I forgot!'

What on earth? His heart pounded as he raced to get to her, and found her shivering at the door of the house.

'I left the cap behind,' she cried out. 'I forgot Jake's peaked cap. But now I can't go back inside again, not today. I can't.'

He brushed a strand of her hair from her face.

'Calm down, sweetheart. I'll fetch it.

You get into the car.'

He handed her the case.

'Would you mind taking this?'

There was a glimmer of a smile behind her tears.

'I don't know why I panicked. Thank you, Nat,' she said simply and, as if in a daze, strolled off towards her car.

As he entered the house, he hoped that today she had finally spent all her emotional turmoil, come to terms with Jake's death. He'd had to, but it was easier for him, because he thought he knew the reasons why Jake had done what he did. Over and over in his mind, he'd re-run the argument they'd had a few days before Jake died. He had questioned his commitment to Blythe and the marriage.

'She's too good for me,' Jake said. 'Suppose, deep down, I'm like the rat who fathered me, and walk out on her? I could. It happens. Sometimes I think there's a real rotten streak in me.'

He'd slapped his hand to his head.

Nat had to drag back the words

which first came to his lips.

'If things go wrong for you, I'll be here to pick up the pieces. No way will Blythe get damaged the way our mother did,' he longed to say but said instead, 'No, Jake, you're wrong. You're suffering pre-wedding nerves. Blokes do. You wouldn't desert Blythe. You've got too much integrity.'

'Mate, the way I feel now, I reckon the smart thing to do is call off the wedding for a year or two. Give myself some space.'

'You've already had four years to satisfy your need for other women, and I've kept quiet. You can't pull out now. Everything's arranged. You'd break the girl's heart, and old Tom's. Believe in yourself. You'll make her a fine husband.'

In the end, Jake had cried, rebuked himself for his weakness and promised, once they were married, he'd change his ways. But, in the lonely, early morning of a few days later, following a bachelor night involving heavy drinking, Jake had stripped off his clothes on the banks of the river, and walked into it.

Nat realised then that he hadn't understood how troubled his brother was about coming from an unhappy, violent union and maybe inheriting his old man's traits. Or his fear that he might fail those who loved him. Nat hadn't understood. Or hadn't wanted to? He groaned. If he'd left well alone, not badgered his brother into going ahead with the wedding, eventually Blythe and Jake would have made it to the altar. And if they hadn't? Marriages fell apart all the time these days.

So often, in his dark, lonely bedroom, he'd wished he'd kept his big mouth shut. He'd replay the scene, re-invent the words, change the outcome, give Jake the courtesy of working out his own destiny. Calling off the wedding would have been infinitely better than losing Jake. His spasms of guilt intensified after Blythe returned home, fanned by the pain and the appeal in her eyes when they reached out to him for answers.

Jake's cap lay on the bedside table. He picked it up, then looked around him, wondering if he would ever get back to this home which had once been his pride. Here, Jake's presence still seemed to pervade everything. Nat had bought and restored the house but, he thought, it was Jake who had brought it to life. Placing Jake's cap on his head while he closed the windows, he left, slamming the front door. He found Blythe huddled in the car's passenger seat.

'Blythe,' he prompted, his voice low, not wishing to startle her.

'Jake?' she whispered. 'Is that you?'

'It's Nat. I've brought you Jake's cap.'

He handed it to her, before making his way in front of the car and around to the driver's seat. There, he climbed in and started up the engine.

Shaken, her thoughts in chaos, Blythe placed the cap on her lap, stretched back in the seat, and closed her eyes.

Thank goodness Nat didn't talk. The silence, the deep breaths she took, helped still her mind. By the time the car stopped in the driveway of home, she'd regained some of her composure. She knew exactly what her next move would be. Nat carried in the box. She clasped the wallet and Jake's cap in her hand as she went straight to her bedroom. He followed and laid the mahogany box and case by her bed. After glancing at her watch, she looked across at him.

'I'd like half an hour alone. Can you hold the fort? Tell Pa I'm fine.'

'Don't hurry. It sounds as if Jack and Tom are still at it. If you're up to it, I'll invite Jack to stay on for dinner.'

She nodded, then she turned her back on Nat, willing him to leave. When she heard him close her door, she flopped on to the bed, and slowly unclipped the wallet. But it held no secrets, gave no hint of his personality. Jake didn't even carry a photograph of her. It was a faceless, empty thing, she thought bitterly. She had been right to expect nothing. The police would have gone through it thoroughly.

Perhaps there was something in the box she'd missed earlier. She raised the lid with uncertain fingers. As she lifted Jake's watch, a gold pen, the cuff links, one by one, her mind sped back to the birthdays and special occasions when he had received them, evoking painful memories of happy events. She straightened her shoulders, tilted her chin, replaced them, and frustrated at her lack of progress, closed the lid a little sharper than necessary. The impact caused Jake's cap, which rested on the bed, to bounce and drop to the floor. A small piece of paper fluttered from beneath its band.

Could this be what she was looking for? Her heart on hold, she bent to retrieve it, and with shaky fingers turned it over. On it were scribbled, a name, Sarah, and a phone number!

6

Blythe's mind hadn't stopped spinning since she found the note. Did the phone number belong to Jake's mother, or to the Sarah she'd met on the boat, the one who claimed to have been out to dinner with Jake? And why was it hidden in the band of his cap? That alone made it suspicious. Should she have mentioned it to Nat?

At last Pa was sleeping. She could make the call without risk of being overheard. She took the phone into her bedroom, closed the door, sat on the bed, and with trembling fingers tapped out the number. A woman with an older voice answered.

'May I speak to Sarah?' Blythe asked, trying to sound relaxed, though her heart pulsed with anxiety.

'I'm sorry, but she's gone back to Melbourne. Is it urgent? My daughter won't be home until the next long weekend.'

At least she knew this Sarah wasn't Jake's mother. That left the Sarah from the river boat.

'Can I say who called?' the woman asked.

An unexpected answer came to Blythe's lips.

'I was a friend of Jake's.'

The woman's voice grew gentle.

'You poor girl. I'm sorry. I suppose he led you on, too.'

Then her voice turned frosty.

'He took my Sarah out a few times then dumped her for someone else. She was terribly upset. She thought he was serious. That's why she went to Melbourne to live. If you ask me, there's something very odd about the way he died.'

'Odd?' Blythe whispered.

'Sarah found out later he had a habit of taking women out and then dumping them. I'm wondering if one of his ex-lady friends caught up with him.'

'You mean . . . ' Blythe gasped.

'You'd better forget I said that. I'm real sorry you've been hurt. I'll get Sarah to call you when she comes home, if you like. You could compare notes. Did you give me your name, dear?'

'I'll ring again,' Blythe managed in a hushed voice as she replaced the phone.

She flicked damp hair from her forehead, her mind churning with questions, desperate for answers, sick at heart. Suddenly she felt terribly alone. Pa was too ill to be told of Jake's duplicity, and her confidante, the one reliable constant in her life, Nat, who must have known, had betrayed her by not telling her about Jake's affairs.

Could Sarah's mother be wrong? In her bitterness over losing her daughter to the city, she may have assumed Jake caused her to leave. But that didn't add up. The woman mentioned other young women in the district who'd been hurt by Jake's cavalier attitude. She'd even gone further, and hinted at murder!

Blythe shuddered. She'd wrapped herself up in a cloak of happiness at being chosen by the district's most sought-after bachelor. She knew how attractive Jake was to other women, yet she'd refused to contemplate that he might flaunt his charm, lead women on, accept their advances, not even when Jenny hinted at it.

Jenny had known. Everyone knew, everyone but her. She paced the house, back and forth to the front window. Would Nat never come home today?

Nat, who knew Jake more intimately than anyone else, had gone on perpetuating the lie that Jake loved her, even after his death. He was as guilty as his brother. She would demand answers, tell him she never wanted to see him again. After the first desperate hour, she pulled her thoughts together sufficiently to form a plan. Nat would come home to a normal household, the dinner prepared, Pa in the sitting room in his wheelchair. She would not assail Nat with questions the minute he stepped inside. She would save her accusations until later, after Pa had been settled.

Yet, when she heard his footsteps around the side of the house, her feet almost took over. She clung to the kitchen bench, taking several deep breaths to steady herself.

Throughout dinner, then a game of Scrabble, getting Pa to bed, too often the desire to lash out at Nat swept over her. But she held on. If she surprised him, she had her best chance of getting him to admit what he knew. At last they were alone. The fire burned cheerfully. Stay calm, Blythe warned herself as she dropped into Pa's chair, from where she could engage Nat's eyes, watch his responses, interpret his body language.

'Out with it, Blythe. What's bugging you?'

He caught her off-guard.

'I don't understand.'

'Something's been worrying you all evening. What have I done?'

Had she been that obvious? She sighed. No point in denying it.

'I found a note tucked into the braid around Jake's cap,' she said.

'What the devil. A note?' His voice rose. 'What kind of note?'

'It had the name Sarah and a phone number on it. I rang the number.'

'Was that wise?'

Annoyed, her voice strengthened.

'Don't you want to know who Sarah is?'

'Not if she's my mother. That's a definite no.'

He kept his eyes averted, but a tinge of red coloured his tanned complexion. She laughed harshly.

'She's one of Jake's many lady friends.'

Her heart went on hold, but Nat turned to the newspaper he was holding and ran his eyes over its front page — or pretended to.

'Suddenly lost your voice? I'm speaking to you, Nat Buchanan,' she said, showing irritation. 'Sarah is one of Jake's lady friends. Just one of them.'

'B C,' he said, folding the paper,

126

finally looking at her.

'I don't understand riddles,' she snapped.

'My little joke. I meant Before Chilli.' His grin didn't get even halfway there.

'You're lying to me, Nat. He played fast and loose with girls for years, and you abetted him in keeping it from me. You, of all people. I trusted you with my life, but not any more.'

Tossing the paper to the floor, he stood up, moving quickly to her side. She felt small, vulnerable, lonely, and wondered if she could go on without weeping.

'Surely you understand he wasn't serious about them. Sure, women threw themselves at him, especially on the boat trips. It's that kind of job. You wear a uniform, you meet women, they're carefree, ready for a holiday fling. I watched him struggle against it, but he was only human. Sometimes the women came on so strongly, he lost the fight.'

'I don't hear you confessing the women threw themselves at you.'

He tilted her chin with his index finger, and tried to smile.

'With Jake around?'

Blythe looked into his dark eyes, pools of concern. There was no mistaking how he felt. He was hurting for her, for his brother. But she felt only confusion.

'And because it was your precious, little brother, you let me go on living in a fool's paradise,' she accused, pushing his hand away.

'Because I knew he loved you dearly. He promised me that once you were married he'd settle down. I trusted him to do that.'

'He promised you? He promised me more than that. We both know now that his promises were worthless.'

'Blythe, a few nights before he died, we talked. He . . . '

She stepped away, overwhelmed by a sudden, appalling thought. She cried out.

'Dear heavens, is it possible he felt so guilty about his affairs that he killed himself? Tell me it's not. I couldn't bear that on my conscience.'

Nat took her into his arms and ran a finger down her tear-stained cheek.

'Hush, now. Of course you weren't to blame. If anyone's at fault, it's me. I should have left well alone. I knew his affairs were fleeting, meaningless, but I wanted to make sure Jake understood. I mean once you were married, I felt confident he wouldn't hurt you.'

She drew away from him.

'You approved of him hurting other women?'

He dashed his hand through his hair.

'No! I'm not excusing him, but you know Jake's history. He missed out on love as a child. Your mother was the only person who showed him any love in his formative years. So, when women reached out to him, he accepted their affection. Is that so unforgivable?'

'Of course it is. I don't see you behaving like that.'

'Who knows what I'd do if women hung around me as they did around him?'

'I know. You'd have sent them packing. Pa was right. You're solid and reliable.'

'You left out boring.'

She gazed steadily at him.

'Nat, you've let me down so badly.'

It wasn't the answer he'd hoped for.

'Maybe you'd prefer me without my Mr Reliable tag. That way I'd remind you more of Jake.'

He raised his voice, unable to curb its mocking tone. Blythe sighed wearily.

'For goodness' sake, this isn't about you. It's about Jake. You know the worst part of this rotten business? He was cheating on me and everyone in town knew, except me. And that includes Jenny. Oh, dear heavens, I've just had a horrible thought. Tell me Pa didn't know.'

She sounded so bitter, so unlike herself. Nat decided indulging her need to lash out wasn't helping.

'Aren't you being a bit over the top? You're shocked. I understand that, but would it really matter if Tom knew?'

'It would to me. He knew, didn't he?' she accused.

'He didn't, but he knew Jake wasn't an angel. He had the good sense to allow him some space because of his background.'

She laughed harshly.

'But you hid his shabby, little affairs from me because you decided I couldn't handle it. Who do you think you are? Isn't it enough that you've made yourself indispensable to Pa. Do you have to go on playing big brother to me?'

'I did what I thought was right.'

'In future I'll make my own decisions. In case you hadn't noticed, I'm a big girl now.'

If he were to follow his instincts he'd take her in his arms, soothe away the hurt that had made her strike out so vehemently at him. But he averted his gaze, tended the fire, tried to think clearly. Where did they go from here? It had become increasingly difficult to live in the same house as Blythe and hide his feelings for her. Yet, if he moved out, who would help her with Tom?

She solved his immediate problem, by saying in a tight, controlled voice, 'I've arranged with Sally Spencer for a district nurse to come in daily while I'm in the city to tie up the loose ends at the office. I'm leaving tomorrow, and will be away three days. Are you all right to stay on until I get back?'

Then she strode to the door not waiting for an answer.

'A break away will do you good,' he called after her.

She swung back to him, her eyes glinting with fire.

'I'm not taking a break away. I have to go on business. When I get back, I expect to find you packed and ready to move out, Nat Buchanan. And convince Pa it's your decision.'

'Aye, aye, Captain Chilli.'

He saluted. He'd meant to ease the

tension, but instead it inflamed her temper.

'Get lost,' she snapped and slammed out of the room.

★   ★   ★

Blythe pushed through the Sydney lunch-time crowds on her way back to her office. Petrol fumes and dust hung in the air. One more session at the computer showing her replacement operator the systems, and she'd be free to return to Murray Bend. The time away from home had turned out to be unexpectedly beneficial.

Without depending on Nat and Pa for reassurance, she'd started to think more clearly, assess where the loss of Jake had left her, and what she wanted to do from here. At close on twenty-five, with a lifetime ahead of her, she'd discovered that in spite of everything, she wanted to return home to her life by the river. But what troubled her most was the fact that she'd treated Nat so unfairly. All these years she'd selfishly taken his attention for granted. Now she felt desperate for his forgiveness. She'd tried to mend their relationship on the phone the previous night.

'I can't believe how self-centred and blind I've been. I let my emotions, my hurt, spill over. It's all so clear to me now. Of course, by not telling me about Jake, you were trying to protect me.'

All he'd said was, 'That's water under the bridge, Blythe. I've informed Tom I'm moving out as soon as you come home. He understands my need to get back to my own place. Jenny made it easy.'

'Jenny?'

'I'll tell you all about it when you get back. Goodnight, Blythe.'

When she returned home would she learn that Nat and Jenny were to marry? Or had married?

She faltered in front of a show window, trying some window-shopping to clear Jenny and Nat out of her mind.

He deserved a woman who put him first, who was thoughtful and caring. But suddenly a reflection in the glass shop front hijacked her attention.

Jake! She drew in her breath, stared. The image faded. She swung around, searching in the throng for the dark-headed figure.

7

The tall figure moved ahead smartly, partly hidden by the crowds. Blythe's heart pounded wildly as her feet carried her forward, knocking into people, forcing them aside as her steps grew longer, more desperate. She ran. He turned a corner, and when Blythe reached it, he had disappeared. She searched wildly in shops, lanes, the adjacent carpark. Tears of frustration filled her eyes. She leaned against a wall, her breath coming in short gasps.

'Are you all right?' a passerby asked.

'Fine.'

She waved the person away, and then forced herself into a nearby coffee shop, where she sat, numb. Through chattering teeth, she ordered coffee. Perhaps for fifteen minutes she remained there, stunned, sipping the coffee, thinking the possibilities. But no matter how deeply she questioned herself, the conviction, the feeling that she had seen Jake refused to go away. And, as her head cleared, the image, the reflection in the shop window, grew stronger in her mind. She recalled clearly now that he carried a supermarket shopping bag.

Blythe could no longer go home tomorrow. She had to find Jake. She decided to call Nat.

'I always seem to be asking favours of you.'

She controlled the tremor in her voice. The need to tell Nat she'd seen Jake was strong, but he'd laugh at her, tell her she was dreaming. However, he sounded more relaxed than he had last night.

'Go for it,' he told her.

'If Pa's feeling all right, I'd like to stay in town for a couple more days. There are a few jobs still to be completed,' she embroidered the truth. 'I know I've got a nerve, but could you do this one last thing for me and stay on for a bit longer?'

'Tom's fine, but I've made arrangements to move out at the weekend. You will be back by then?'

'Of course.'

She tried to sound light-hearted, though she felt flat. She missed him. She longed to beg him to stay on, and he hadn't even gone. She wasn't even home and already she knew she'd miss him like crazy. But until she discovered if Jake were alive, nothing would ever be the same again. All her insecurities re-emerged. Reasons for Jake's disappearance flashed through her head. He didn't love her? He had another woman? He was in financial trouble? She wanted to curl up in a ball and sleep away the hurt of being so harshly rejected.

Next day, having completed her contract with her employer, and packed her belongings from the flat, she returned to the area where she'd seen Jake. There, she took a room at a nearby motel and lingered along the shopping strip in the hope of glimpsing him again. If he lived or worked in the area, chances were he shopped there regularly.

On Thursday morning, her final day in town, as she had done the last couple of days, she pushed a broad-brimmed hat on her head, turned up the collar of her shirt, and bought a newspaper. Then she made her way to the seat on the footpath outside the supermarket and waited. But by twelve-thirty she began to stop hoping he'd show up, until she remembered it was around this time of day when Jake, if it was him, appeared three days ago.

She sat on, thankful that the late winter sun had found its way to her seat, warming her, hopefully explaining her sunglasses and shady hat to any casual observer. She'd have killed for a coffee, but dare not leave her post. This was her last opportunity to locate Jake. If she didn't, her conscience told her she'd have to report her sighting to the police at Murray Bend.

Then her pulse started to race, her

hands sweated. It was him! She raised the newspaper to cover her face, but not her eyes. He wore a navy T-shirt. As he neared, she saw how his jeans outlined his fit, muscular body, his familiar walk, somewhere between a stroll and a swagger. He was alone. Peeping over the newspaper, she noticed his dark hair had grown. His jawline was shadowed by a few days' growth, and he, too, wore sunglasses. She may have had doubts over this man's identity, if she hadn't known his walk so intimately, the cut of his body, the width of his shoulders.

Jake Buchanan was alive!

She'd thought about this moment so often in the last couple of days, thought she knew exactly how she would react. She'd confront him, beat on his body with tight fists, denounce him with the energy of a hungry cat on the kill. But her body let her down. She remained seated, trembling, as the chill in her heart spread to her limbs. She allowed him to stride on unchallenged, and disappear into a real estate agency a few doors from the supermarket.

Blythe sat on, afraid to rise lest her legs fold beneath her, her concentration captive to the agency door, waiting for Jake to reappear. If only Nat were here, he'd know what to do. But she'd been relying on Nat to fix things for her all her life. This problem was hers. Slowly the sun penetrated her chilled body, her limbs warmed. She could move again.

Impatient, she glanced at her watch. Fifteen minutes, and still no Jake. Could he have left by another entrance? She folded the newspaper, deciding to investigate, but before she could stand up, he strolled from the estate agency. From her vantage point he appeared to be smiling. Hastily she reopened the newspaper, and behind it watched him retrace his steps. He was coming back to the supermarket. Her hands trembled as they clutched the paper, raising it higher. But he strolled into the supermarket without even glancing in her direction.

Blythe filled her parched lungs with air, and dumping the newspaper into a handy waste basket, hurried towards the estate agency. Breathing quickly, she approached the man behind the counter.

'I was supposed to meet my partner here about twenty minutes ago, but was held up.'

Then she drew a photograph of Jake from her wallet, held it towards the assistant and offered the widest smile she could manage.

'He's changed a bit from this picture. He wears his hair longer now.'

'Mr Neil Jacobs? What a pity. You've just missed him. If you hurry you might catch him up.'

Her heart quickened.

'I'm dying to know how he got on. Were you able to help us?'

'Yes. He's taken the flat you were interested in at Drummoyne.'

The assistant handed her an advertising leaflet from the desk. Glancing at it, Blythe noticed several of the properties were in the same area.

'We liked two of them. Which one did he decide on?'

Blythe amazed herself. Her questioning sounded so natural.

'This one.'

He indicated the property on the page.

'He paid a security fee and three months' rent. He thought you'd approve. I hope you like it.'

'Fantastic. So when can we move in?'

'Not until next week. The present tenant still has things to move out.'

She folded the leaflet with shaky fingers, tucked it into the pocket of her trousers, then, about to leave, she turned back.

'I'd like to surprise Neil when I meet him, by telling him I've seen the house again. I think I'll drive by. I'll recognise it from the sketch on the leaflet, won't I?'

'You can't miss it. It has large, bay windows. But you understand you can't go in, of course.'

'You've been very helpful. Thank you.'

She turned swiftly and hurried out, expecting at any moment to feel a heavy hand fall on her shoulder and to hear the words, 'Madam, you're under arrest for false pretences.'

Outside, hat in hand, her legs flying, Blythe made it to her motel room, breathless to read the leaflet, breathless to work out her next move. She switched on the kettle, threw her bag and hat on to the table and reached into her pocket for the property leaflet. As she unfolded it, she felt a sense of satisfaction. She'd been enterprising. In a million years she wouldn't have thought it possible she had the audacity and cunning to glean the information she'd acquired.

The house at Drummoyne over-looked the harbour. Expensive, she thought. That was Jake. He liked the best and even convinced her that he could have it simply by being Jake. All these years she'd been blinded by the gloss of his charm, his adventurous attitude towards life, his romanticism. Even when she recognised his weaknesses, she'd excused them on his childhood without love, as Nat had. But in one sense Jake had been truly blessed, for he'd had Nat's love, Nat's single-minded attention and devotion.

She made a cup of coffee, and pacing, tried to work out where to go from here. One thing she was clear about. She wouldn't involve Nat. She'd tackle Jake alone. Swept up in restless energy, she planned to go to his Drummoyne flat, knock on the door. She imagined the look on his face, his stuttering explanation. She'd laugh as he squirmed and suffered.

Her mood shifted. She'd see again his brilliant blue eyes, be once more captivated by his wide smile. She put her head into her hands to shut out the image. Then, drawing on her new-found determination, she tilted her chin. This time she would be the winner. The man didn't love her, probably never had, and that hurt.

She didn't want to rethink the pain, to revisit the numbing emptiness he'd left behind, the demeaning loss of pride as she returned the wedding presents, to see and feel the pity in the eyes of the local people. And yet it was the only way she knew to work up her anger. This man had faked his death in a cold, premeditated way and absconded, leaving her behind, leaving her family behind, to grieve for him. And, for whatever reason, he had to pay.

But she couldn't seek retribution until next week when Jake moved to the Drummoyne address. That meant waiting around, days of inactivity, which would dull her anger, ease her desire to see him suffer. There had to be something she could do now. Think, she urged herself, think. Suddenly the phone rang. She jumped, but let it shrill on as she sipped her coffee, fuelling her anger with her thoughts.

When she finally knocked on his door and poured out her contempt, her hurt, she had to be fired up with fury, certain that loving him had been a momentous mistake. Only after confronting him could she unravel herself from the invisible cord which had laced her to him since childhood.

On and on her thoughts went, tangling, untangling, until at last she acknowledged she had to go home. She'd return to town next week after Jake shifted into the rental flat at Drummoyne. The idea of home, of being with Pa and Nat, eased her mind. She longed to be with them. Having made the decision, her head cleared, and she realised the answer to tracing Jake's present address was to employ a private detective. Again a surge of energy charged through her. She'd borrow a copy of the yellow pages phone directory from the motel office, look one up and get him on the job. She was about to swing into action when heavy knocking sounded on the door.

Her heartbeat accelerated. Jake was never far from her thoughts. She shook her head, told herself not to be paranoid. It couldn't be him! The female proprietor stood on the doorstep.

'Miss Neilsen, there's a distance phone call in my office for you. Apparently the caller couldn't get through to you here.'

Blythe hung on to the door's edge.

'Really? I've been here.'

'Yes, I noticed you come in. Are you all right? You look pale.'

'I'm fine, thanks. Tired, I guess.'

'I'll switch the call through. There's no need for you to come out.'

'I was about to come over, anyway. I want to borrow the yellow pages, if I may. I can't imagine who the call is from.'

'I wouldn't have troubled you, but he said it's urgent.'

Blythe's footsteps faltered.

'Urgent?' she whispered, knowing the caller had to be Nat — knowing instinctively there was something wrong.

Knowing Pa was ill, she raced ahead of the manager, reached the reception room and seized up the handset.

'Nat,' she cried. 'Is that you, Nat? What's wrong with Pa?'

'Blythe, he's had another heart attack. No need to panic, but he wants to see you. Can you drop everything and get back today?'

'Of course I can. What happened? He will be all right, won't he?'

Her voice trembled.

'Sure he will, once he sees you. He's at the hospital. I've booked you on the three o'clock flight this afternoon. Pick up your ticket at the check-in, and leave your car at the long-term carpark. Jenny will meet you at the airport. I'd come myself, but I want to stay by Tom's side.'

In a fog of anxiety, Blythe found herself on the plane, in Jenny's car at Murray Bend, silent, afraid to ask the hard questions, speeding towards the hospital. Into the silence, she at last asked, 'When did it happen?'

'Around mid-day. The nurse had just given him his shower. When you see him, don't be alarmed. He's hooked up to machines and things, but he's conscious, and asking for you.'

Nat looked up when they entered the room, and whispered to Tom.

'Chilli's here, old friend. I'll leave you alone with your Pa, sweetheart,' he added, holding Blythe briefly, putting his lips to her cold cheek.

'Stay,' she whispered. 'He needs us both, Nat.'

She took Nat's seat close to the bedside and placed her hand in Tom's.

'Thank you, love,' the old man mouthed.

Nat strained to hear his next words, as Blythe moved closer, but he failed. Blythe nodded, pushed a wisp of hair back from the old man's face and bent to kiss him on the forehead. An unnatural stillness claimed the room as if time had ceased to tick by.

Then Blythe cried out, 'Pa, don't go. There's so much I have to tell you. I love you. I need you. Don't go.'

Only then did Nat realise the machine no longer showed Tom's heartbeat. He stormed out to the nurses' station, calling for help, but the emergency team arrived too late to revive the old man.

Nat and Blythe sat silently at his bedside. Nat knew not for how long. How did you say goodbye to the man who had been better than a father to you? How did you comfort his grand-daughter, when you were in need of comfort yourself?

For days to follow, the lonely Becky Em rode the gentle tides, moored to the little jetty. People called at the Neilsen house expressing their sympathy. The local paper covered Captain Tom's funeral, and wrote affectionately of his love of the river, the early paddle-steamers and the people of his town.

'Tom wouldn't have wanted any fuss,' Nat told the newspaper reporter who interviewed him, 'but it's timely to remind people of the history of our river and the men who respected it and learned to live with its unpredictability.'

Though Nat was kept busy with arrangements, Blythe sometimes saw his dark eyes glisten with tears, sometimes glance over photographs or a book Pa had been reading, looking at his chair in its soul-searing emptiness. She suspected he kept any show of grief for private moments, because she needed his strength, his support. She alternated between picking at her food, wandering around the house as if lost, and bursts of energy when she went through cupboards or cleaned and scrubbed Pa's room.

A week after the funeral, Blythe came into the kitchen, exhausted after her latest cleaning effort. Nat was preparing lunch.

'I let Pa down,' she said, taking up a knife and slicing through sandwiches. 'Why was I never here when he needed me?'

Nat turned dark, concerned eyes to her.

'Don't do this to yourself, sweetheart. You brought him so much joy after your father and mother died. You kept him and Becky going, gave them something to live for. Besides, no-one can predict when people will die. You rang him every day. He knew you were thinking about him. And it's not as if you were off having fun. You were working.'

Tears welled in her eyes. As she dropped into a chair, her hands trembled. Nat had it wrong. She could have come home earlier, but, no, she'd been thinking of herself, hunting down Jake with vengeance in her heart. Nat came to her, removed the knife from her hands and folded them into his.

'He'd want you to forget the bad times and be happy. He watched with great pride and admiration as you struggled and won after we lost Jake.'

Suddenly, the fog through which she'd processed all her feelings since Jake's death cleared.

'Of course I haven't won. If I had, I

wouldn't give a damn about Jake, but I do,' she cried.

'I understand, but you've made good progress. And I'm here for you.'

She wrenched her hands away, laughing mirthlessly.

'You haven't got a clue. I feel disgust, contempt for the man. But I can't let it rest. I need to confront him once more, make him feel my pain.'

Her outburst surprised her, but she managed to contain the simmering urge to tell Nat that she'd discovered Jake was still alive. In the context of Pa's death it became unimportant. But when Nat mentioned his name just now her desire to make Jake pay for the unhappiness and misery he'd meted out to this family surfaced.

Nat gently brushed back her hair from her face.

'Tom's happy now. No more struggling to make an effort for us.'

He tilted her chin.

'Come on. I want to see those eyes of yours start shining again with hope for the future. There's so much to look forward to.'

'But I'm not ready to move on. There's something I have to settle first. And it's not for Pa. It's for me.'

'You do know that even if you'd been around, Tom would have died. He's been on borrowed time for months. His heart was worn out. He told me more than once he looked forward to meeting up with his Becky, and Jake.'

Nat turned back to the bench, muttering something under his breath. He's growing impatient with me, she thought. He still thinks it upsets me to hear Jake's name.

'Look, it doesn't hurt any more when you mention Jake. I meant what I said just now. I feel only contempt for him.'

'Yeah? Since when?'

In a flash, she realised facing Jake alone was self-indulgent. Shutting out Nat wasn't fair. She had to tell him his brother was alive. He had a right to know, and to decide what to do with the information. She began slowly.

'There's something I have to say, Nat, but you'd better sit down.'

When he made no response, either by word or movement, she raised her voice slightly.

'Will you sit down? I'm not being dramatic. This is about as serious as it gets.'

'Well, what are you waiting for. Spit it out.'

'Jake's alive.'

He dropped the knife he was using, spun around, lowered his eyebrows.

'Did I hear you correctly?' he demanded.

'I said, Jake's alive,' she repeated.

'Damn it, you're not still hanging on to that idea.'

'It's not an idea. It's the truth. I've seen him.'

He retrieved the knife, rinsed it under the tap, and kept on with the sandwich making as if he hoped that by ignoring her statement, it might go away.

'You can pretend you didn't hear

what I said, but it won't change anything.'

But he looked so taut with emotion, her heart reached out to him. She went to his side, touched his arm.

'I actually saw him in the city,' she said gently.

8

You saw Jake in the city? Where?' Nat demanded, disbelief written right across his ashen face.

'In a busy shopping mall. I was window-shopping when I saw his reflection in the glass,' she explained.

Blythe sounded convincing, strong in her belief. Yet Nat's doubts persisted.

'A reflection? You probably imagined it.'

'I wasn't sure at first, but before you ridicule me any more, hear the remainder of my evidence, please.'

He heaved his shoulders, uncertain how to handle this turn of events.

'I'm listening,' he said.

'After I saw his reflection, I tried to catch up with him, but he disappeared into the lunchtime crowds.'

'And that's it?'

'No,' she went on, 'that's not it.

Listen to what I'm saying. Your brother is alive. He's a cheat and a deceiver. He arranged his disappearance, of that I'm certain. And now that we know, we have to deal with it.'

Nat's doubts fell away. It had to be true. Though the enormity of what his brother had done rendered him numb, a tiny ray of happiness shone through it. He couldn't switch off his love for his younger brother.

'OK, you have my undivided attention,' he said quietly, leaning against the bench. 'Go on. Tell me everything. I won't interrupt again.'

Her fingers wrapped around his arm.

'You're bowled over by this. Why don't we sit down? I was so busy counting my loss, seeing things from my point of view, I forgot about your feelings and how much Jake meant to you. And now that you know he's still alive, what on earth are you thinking?'

She smiled up at him, her lovely eyes soft with concern, as she took his hand and led him to the sofa in the living room. After sitting, she wriggled close to him. Their bodies touched.

'Would you hold me, while I tell you everything?' she asked, slipping beneath his arm.

Her head against his chest unsettled him even more. At this moment, he marvelled at the fact that it was she who had all the strength. She had become the comforter, the protector. She had grown, was dealing with the fact that Jake was alive. He wasn't. Holding her, slightly dazed, he spoke huskily.

'I'm fine. Go on, Blythe.'

'The day after I saw Jake, I went back to the same area in the hope that he might reappear. I figured there was a real chance he'd return to that same supermarket, so I prepared to spend a few days waiting, in case he showed.'

'You've been watching those lady detective TV shows,' he said, trying to ease the tension in his body.

'It worked, though. That's all that matters.'

Blythe related how she'd seen Jake again, of her visit to the estate agency, how she'd tricked her way into getting the address of the flat Jake had leased in Drummoyne. Finally, she dug Nat gently in the ribs, glanced up with a smug smile.

'Now, say I imagined it all.'

'You did well.'

She edged away from his hold, her eyes searching his for some response.

'Can't you do any better than that? Confess, I did brilliantly.'

'I'm still trying to process what you've told me. How did you feel, Blythe? Hurt? Furious? Tell me?'

'I used to think if I could find Jake again, it wouldn't matter what he'd done. I'd be over the moon to have him back. That's all I wanted. But without knowing it, my feelings have changed. When I saw him on the street, instead of throwing myself at him, I seethed with anger. I physically ached with it. I wanted revenge. I planned to go knocking on his door and really stitch him up. But then Pa died and my anger eased. And now I'm not sure how to proceed. What do you think, Nat? Should I seek my half hour of retribution and hope it satisfies me, or forget he exists?'

He caressed damp hair back from her forehead.

'Honestly? I just don't know what to suggest. You're the one he hurt most. But what's eating away at me is the knowledge that if the police find out, he could go to prison.'

'You mean he'd be charged with something?' she cried. 'I didn't think of that. I've stopped loving him, but seeing him in prison, it sounds horrendous. We're the only people he's hurt. Maybe himself because he's lost his family. But honestly, the terrible emptiness and the anger I felt have almost disappeared.'

'It comes down to this. Could you forgive him, Blythe?'

He placed his lips to her burning cheek.

'Not exactly. I think locating him has

helped, though. Don't ask me why. Maybe because I no longer have to live with the idea that he killed himself rather than face marriage to me. There I go again, thinking only of myself.'

She gazed up at him.

'Nat, tell me how you feel. You were the best brother to him. You loved him so much.'

'I was a lousy brother. I blame myself for his weakness. Tom used to tell me I excused his cavalier behaviour too often. If I'd been tougher, he might have squared up to his responsibilities like a man. But I kept on defending him. He had the best girl in the world, and he walked away.'

He thumped his thigh with one hand.

'Damn it, Blythe, he had so much to look forward to. What on earth drove him to fake his death?'

Nat released her, surged to his feet, full of anger.

'You mustn't blame yourself. I'm convinced now he was never in love with me. But he couldn't face telling me or Pa.'

Her voice faltered and her eyes shone with tears as Nat went on.

'Or me. Don't absolve me. I insisted he go ahead with the marriage. That night we talked, he suggested postponing things for a year. I put it down to pre-wedding nerves. I was blind to his true feelings.'

'Because you didn't want me hurt.'

He laughed mockingly.

'He used to call me Saint Nathaniel. That's me, only this time things went terribly wrong. If you're looking for someone to blame, I'm your man. If we hadn't had that heart-to-heart . . . '

She reached out, touching his arm gently and urged him back to the sofa.

'Nat, you have to stop taking on other people's responsibilities. More and more I'm learning that adults have to accept responsibility for their actions. If we must apportion blame, it rests with the family as a whole. Looking at it from Jake's perspective, he must have felt we'd ganged up on him. We all wanted this marriage. He didn't, and it's clear now, he was right.'

'You're making excuses for him and me.'

She tucked her legs under her body, then rested her head on the back of the sofa as if tired, recalling with a soft voice, 'You know, in the years we went out together, I had these twinges of unease. I saw the way he looked at other girls, and wondered, but not for long. He knew how to romance a woman.'

'He could have taught me a thing or two about women, eh?' Nat said ironically.

Another small smile curved her lips.

'I doubt it. You're different from your brother — thoughtful, caring.'

'Go on — dependable, dull,' he chimed in, reluctant to hear the damning words fall from her lovely lips.

'I don't think you realise how attractive you are, Nat Buchanan.'

'Don't stop there,' he said, grinning.

'If you're fishing for more compliments, forget it.'

Her mouth tightened again, the brief moment of levity over too soon.

'What are we going to do, Nat?'

'If it's hurting you, we can leave it for now.'

'My pride's still slightly fragile, but we can't put things off any longer. Do we go in search of Jake? Do we inform the police?'

She shivered briefly and he drew her close.

'I haven't got the answers. I'm torn, Blythe. If Jake went to prison . . . '

She shivered again.

'I don't want to alarm you, Blythe, but we have to be very clear about this. The police spent time and resources searching for him. If we locate Jake, we can't avoid reporting the fact that he's alive to the authorities. What in the name of fortune are we to do? Help me here, Blythe. He's such a free spirit and he could be locked up.'

She looked up at him with imploring eyes.

'You're right. We'd have to report him. But prison? I couldn't bear being responsible for that. If we forget what we know, we wouldn't have to tell anybody that he's alive, would we? It could be our secret.'

He stared at her.

'Could you live with that after all the grief he's given you? Let him go free? Never tell a living soul?'

'I'm willing to try, if you are.'

Suddenly, she leaped to her feet.

'Nat, we don't have to make a decision straight away. Why don't we go down to the Becky Em, get her ready to sail again on Saturday. The fresh air might help us to think clearly.'

She tugged at his hand and he shrugged.

'It's the best idea you've had all day. I'll get the keys and hats. Can you parcel up the sandwiches?'

It was mid-afternoon, getting towards the hottest part of the day. Blythe wore a sun-top and shorts. The sun bit into her bare arms and legs as they sprawled on the floor of the upper deck eating sandwiches, drinking mugs of tea.

'Time for another visit to the hairdresser,' she said, as she reached up and flicked Nat's wide-brimmed hat with her fingers.

He smiled. He'd never smiled at her so. It wasn't warmth. It had a special quality, as if he saw right into her heart, and knew that it beat with a wild, disturbing rhythm, knew that a strange, different need of him surged over her. Her cheeks flushed. She pressed her straw hat on to her head and told herself she imagined it. But somehow, her spirits rose. She felt free.

'Want more sunscreen on your arms?' he asked.

She cast her eyes over her exposed arms and legs.

'I think I should move into the shade.'

He rose, offering his arms to help her up. His hands felt slightly abrasive, work toughened, hard, masculine, yet sensitive, intimate. Heat coursed through her. She had found him too late.

'How's Jenny? Do you have any plans?' she asked, flopping on to a bench seat under a canvas canopy.

He leaned against the boat's rail, his back to the water.

'Did she tell you something at the funeral? I'm not sure what you mean by plans.'

If Nat and Jenny were planning anything momentous, he'd have told her. She tucked strands of hair under her hat.

'Eloping, for example.'

She laughed shakily.

'We're just waiting for the right moment. These last few days I haven't been able to get away from you long enough to finalise the arrangements.'

His chortle, his carefree, teasing reply didn't reassure her. Blythe regretted she'd opened the subject of Jenny. It cast a shadow over the afternoon. She had never understood the relationship Nat had with Jenny, and he always hedged about it. Soon he would declare himself. She tried to remain positive.

'Don't you dare go off without consulting me. You do know Pa's last words to me were, 'Look after Nat, won't you, Chilli? He needs you'.'

'Yeah? Son-of-a-gun, he said that? And what did you say?'

'I promised I would, but I'm highly amused by the idea that Nat Buchanan needs anyone in his life.'

'He was a smart man, old Tom.'

He gazed down at her. She felt a stirring in her body which totally unnerved and yet excited her. How was it that she had never really looked into her heart and seen this tall, dark man before with untamed hair, the strength of Solomon, the vulnerability of a man who cares too much? How was it she hadn't noticed the invitation in his eyes? Her heartbeat hammered off-key. She averted her eyes.

'I guess we'd better get down to

work. Poor old Becky Em's gathered some dust during her lay-off. I'll get the cleaning equipment.'

She took the ladder-like steps to go below, but turned to tell him he should concentrate on the engine, and collided with his large frame as he followed her. He steadied her, lifted her chin, forced her to meet his dark, intense gaze. His arms reached out to her, folded her to him. Then his lips found hers. Her hat fell from her head as he murmured her name into her hair. She laced her arms about his neck, enticed his lips to hers again, closed her eyes. And the mists which had shrouded her vision to the splendour of Nat, the man, lifted.

Beguiled by Jake, in love with being in love, now she experienced the depths, the heights to which truly being in love could transport and overwhelm you. She indulged herself in the enchantment of being in Nat's arms, of knowing he loved her — until guilt caught up with her.

'Nat, dearest Nat,' she whispered, her

hand caressing the nape of his neck, 'this isn't right. We've forgotten Jenny.'

He brushed her cheek.

'Blythe, is it possible you could love me?'

Blythe sighed deeply.

'I've discovered you too late.'

She placed her hand over his, prolonging his touch, afraid this might be their first and final moment together.

'Too late for what?'

'You and Jenny. I thought by now . . . You talked about eloping.'

'You and I talked about eloping. I was joking. I thought you were, too.'

'I wasn't sure. I mean, I was too afraid to ask.'

'While you were in the city, Jen and I discussed our relationship, and decided its only future lay in remaining good friends.'

'She's a fine person, Nat. I think she loved you.'

'She wants a man who can give her security, dependability, honesty, the things she didn't get from her husband. That's why she was attracted to me. But in the end she decided I wasn't the right person because she knew I've always loved you.'

'She knew? So why was I so slow to find out?'

He kissed her nose.

'Because I worked very hard to hide it from you before Jake disappeared.'

'And since he's been gone?'

She set his arms around her waist, moved closer.

'I've been waiting, daring to hope. You are telling me you love me? You want me?'

'I've grown up, and I love you with all my heart, Nat Buchanan. I want to spend the rest of my life with you. When can we be married?'

He kissed her gently.

'There's one more impediment before we're free to indulge ourselves. I don't think we're going to be able to keep Jake's secret. Eventually one of us will want to get at the truth. It could come between us, cause friction, insecurity. We have to decide what to do about that.'

She nodded.

'Why don't we pay him a visit and talk it through with him? We can decide then what to do.'

9

Blythe and Nat left early on Saturday morning by car for Sydney, their happiness marred only by what lay ahead. They'd chosen the weekend as the best time to find Jake at home, and Jenny and Curley had agreed to do a scaled-down schedule of runs on the Becky Em during their absence.

By two o'clock they were driving slowly along James Street, Drummoyne. Minutes later Blythe clutched Nat's arm.

'That's it,' she almost shrieked, 'the one with the bay windows. Slow down.'

He pulled the car into the kerbside beyond the house of their destination.

'Are you sure you want to do this, sweetheart? I could go in by myself,' he said looking down at her with concern.

'We're a team. We go together, or not at all.'

'And we play it by ear?'

He took her hand as they crossed the road.

'You're a bit shaky,' he said.

'I'll get over it.'

They climbed a steep set of steps to the front door, and Nat pressed the door bell. They could hear it tingling inside, hear light footsteps.

A friendly female voice called, 'Come in if you're good-looking.'

Nat looked at Blythe.

'Is Neil at home? We're friends,' he called.

The door swung open. An attractive, young woman stood there, but the welcoming smile faded.

'Oh,' she stuttered. 'I was expecting Sue and Rob.'

Nat stepped forward quickly, in case she closed the door, and put out his hand.

'Nat Buchanan,' he said, 'and this is Blythe Neilsen, my fiancée. We're old friends of Ja . . . I mean Neil. We've come up from the Murray River Basin.'

'Buchanan?'

She stumbled over the word, paled and didn't see Nat's offered hand.

'You'd better come in.'

She led them into a large room, sparsely furnished and overlooking the harbour.

'Please, sit down.'

Tears weren't far away as her voice trembled.

'I'll call Neil on the mobile. He's down by the water.'

'We can come back later,' Blythe offered, feeling unhappy at the pressure the woman was under.

As she looked at Jake's beautiful woman, the one he'd left her for, Blythe felt only compassion.

'Best you wait,' she whispered before hurrying from the room.

Blythe raised her eyebrows as she and Nat stood together looking out on the water.

'She knows. Jake must have told her,' she whispered.

'At least he hasn't deceived her.'

The young woman returned. Her eyes glistened, as if she'd been crying.

'He's coming right up. Can I offer you coffee, tea, a drink?'

It had grown very warm outside. They opted for a cool drink, and the woman escaped again, dabbing at her eyes, but the drinks didn't arrive. They watched her go down the steps to the road and disappear.

'She hasn't run out on us, has she?' Blythe asked.

'More likely she's gone to warn Jake.'

Moments later, Jake appeared alone and took the stairs to the house two at a time. His enthusiasm, so much a part of his character, now seemed all wrong. He should have been upset that he'd been found out, but it looked as if he intended to brazen it out.

'Nat, Blythe,' he called, storming into the room and seizing Nat in a hug. 'Nat, old mate. It's so good to see you. I've missed you.'

'And you,' Nat said. 'You look good.'

Jake shadow-boxed with him.

'I am mate, and you, big brother, look a ball of muscle.'

Blythe felt puzzled, angry that Jake appeared to be toughing it out, until she noticed the sweat on his brow. He turned to her then.

'What can I say, Blythe, except there hasn't been a day go by when I haven't thought of you, wanted to call you, ask you to forgive me.'

'You seem to be doing rather well without my forgiveness. And you should include your brother in that. He took your disappearance real hard.'

She stopped herself before she got too wound up.

'It's understandable you're bitter,' he said quietly.

'I'm not bitter. Not any more. And we haven't come to harangue you. We've come to ask what you propose to do.'

'Sit down, please. I've got someone I want you to meet and then we can talk. I want Kylie to be here. She knows everything.'

When he returned, he had the lovely young woman with him, holding a baby.

'Meet my wife, Kylie, and my son, Nathaniel Thomas. He's seven, or is it eight months, darling?' he said, putting his arm around her, picking up the soft, tiny hand of little Nat. 'Now you can see why I let everyone down at Murray Bend.'

'Yours?' Blythe gasped.

'Yeah. Isn't he a great little kid? Can you guys stay on? I want to tell you everything. I've been dreading this day, but it's so good to see you, and I'm glad it's over at last.'

'First, we'll give you our news. Blythe and I are engaged,' Nat said.

'Mate, that's about the best news I could have. My two favourite people engaged, eh? I reckon it was in the cards.'

Jake sat on the edge of his chair.

'Well, you're looking for answers, so here goes. When I met Kylie on the Becky Em I was wiped out. I tried not to give in, but she did things to me. I wanted to tell you that night we talked, Nat, that she was having my baby, but it was so damned hard. I knew you'd be furious. It seemed easier to disappear. I thought everyone would forget pretty soon. Kylie kept urging me to contact you and go to the police, but life was going so well. I've got a great job as promotions manager with a sports club, and I couldn't risk losing my beautiful wife and baby. But I reckon I've done a lot of growing up this last twelve months, thanks to Kylie. She's teaching me to be a man.'

★   ★   ★

Blythe and Nat married at a quiet ceremony on board their boat. Tom's old army mates came, and Jenny was Blythe's maid-of-honour. Curley took the helm. Jake and Kylie decided to stay in the city, but Jake agreed to report his deception to the police. At their request, he waited until after their wedding.

'What's the newspaper say?' Blythe asked when Nat arrived home with it under his arm.

Grim-faced, he said, 'Sit down.'

Her stomach knotted. Jake had matured, and she didn't want his wife and baby to suffer.

'Surely he hasn't been sentenced to prison!'

Nat kissed her. She folded herself into his arms and almost forgot about Jake. He tapped her on the nose with the paper.

'The charge of making a false claim to the police has been upheld. Jake's been sentenced to community service once a month. He can do it in the city.'

Blythe threw her arms around Nat, and wondered how she could possibly have thought Jake exciting, romantic, his blue eyes attractive. When Nat gazed at her with his dark eyes she melted into his arms.

After the news of Jake's reappearance broke in Murray Bend, for a short time crowds queued at the booking office to get on to a trip on the Becky Em. They gossiped about the dashing young Jake Buchanan who faked his death for love, after meeting the love of his life on the river boat, as dramatised in the local paper.

Sometimes Blythe caught them looking at her, the woman scorned, with pity in their eyes. If only they felt her strength, the joy, the love that had come into her life once she'd found her beloved Nat.

Soon the headlines about Jake Buchanan gave way to Christmas stories, a heatwave, the water shortage, the international tennis and cricket tournaments. Blythe and Nat kept in touch with Jake, visited the city, supported Jake and his family through the tough times, assured that he had found happiness and peace with Kylie and little Nat.

And before long, they found themselves waiting impatiently for a family of their own!